STRIP SEARCH

ERIN MCCARTHY

Cover art by Hang Le

Connect with Erin:

Twitter

Facebook

Goodreads

www.erinmccarthy.net

ONE

LOOKING out into the crowd of screaming women, Axl Moore felt like the all-you-can-eat buffet at Sizzler and no one had taken a meal in days.

Not that he was complaining.

He wasn't an attention whore on a regular day but for the second annual Tap That charity event he had to admit it didn't suck to have women think he was hot. He and his best friends, Rick, Jesse, and Brandon hadn't even taken the stage yet for their so-called dance routine. AKA hip thrusting and winking.

"I'm so getting laid tonight," Jesse said, as they stood just off-stage. He was tossing a hockey puck up and down in his hands.

Given that Jesse was a pro hockey player, Axl was pretty sure he was getting laid most nights. But it was a requirement in their twenty-year friendship that Axl give Jesse shit. "Not with your dancing skills," he ribbed him.

Jesse snorted. "Okay, I can admit that I can't dance. But you won't be getting laid with your charm either, asshole. You need to work on your game face."

"This isn't a game." Axl held handcuffs in his hand, his

Beaver Bend police department uniform feeling tighter than usual. His phone buzzed in his pocket and he pulled it out.

A text from his mother.

Maybe you'll meet a nice girl tonight. Remember to smile!

That actually made him laugh. He showed the text to his friends. "Jesse, are you in a conspiracy with my mom? Or do you just think like a girl?"

Brandon laughed. "Dude, I don't know what's funnier. That your mother thinks the only thing holding you back is a lack of a smile, or that she thinks a Magic Mike knock-off show with total amateurs in small-town Minnesota is the place to meet a forever girl."

"You mean it's not?" he asked, sarcastically. "Perfectly fine with me because I have no plans for a forever girl." Marriage was not on his bucket list.

"I wouldn't be so quick to dismiss it," Rick said. "You never know who is out there in the crowd tonight. Look at me and Sloane."

Rick had hooked up with Sloane O'Toole after this event the year before, much to the chagrin of their other buddy Sullivan, who happened to be Sloane's brother. "You fucked your best friend's hot older sister. I don't think I can top that." Nor did he want to.

"Hey. We're still going strong a year later. That could be you next year." Rick gave him a grin.

"I wouldn't bet your auto body shop on it. Because you'll lose." Axl was the very definition of content. He liked being alone, even if no one else, and sometimes even he, didn't understand why. He enjoyed women. He appreciated their soft skin, and their curves, and light, sweet voices. He thought women were amazing creatures that occasionally he got to touch.

But he knew women had emotional expectations and needs

and generally speaking, he would fail to live up to them because he wasn't Rick, who laughed easily and had been in love with Sloane from the age of fifteen. Or Sullivan, who had loved his wife Kendra since high school, and was still devastated from her death.

Then there was Jesse fully enjoying being single. If anyone, Brandon might get where Axl was coming from, but at the same time, Brandon was a serious and accomplished flirt, and he was more the "you, me, my place," kind of guy.

He scanned the crowd, casually. Amused that it seemed like every woman in Beaver Bend was at the bar, from twenty-one year old Rachel Ryder to Mrs. Dobish, who was ninety if she was a day. In her wheelchair, wearing a hot pink cardigan, she was waving a twenty. Damn.

Lilly, the choreographer, spoke into a microphone. "Hey, everyone! Give a warm welcome to our Tap That Dancers, back for our second annual Breast Cancer Awareness Event! Let's hear it for the boys!"

The crowd roared. The music started. Axl felt nothing more than casual amusement, entertained by the break in his normal day-to-day routine. He stepped onto stage.

The room was a sea of familiar faces, the hallmark of small-town life. Most women were in jeans and T-shirts or clingy silky shirts and were women he recognized.

"Introduce yourselves, guys," Lilly said, holding the mic to each of them in turn. "Tell us something we would never guess about you."

"I'm Axl," he said, twirling the handcuffs on his index finger. "But you can call me Officer Moore."

"Oooh, more what?" Lilly asked, giving him a grin.

"More of everything."

The women screamed even louder and he smirked at the idea that somewhere out there in the throng was a forever girl.

Jesse had the right idea. If ever there was a perfect opportunity to get laid, this was it.

The door opened and a blonde wearing a dress, her generous curves outlined gloriously in it, slipped into the bar.

The night just got a whole lot more interesting.

"YOU HAVE TO BRING IT," Sadie Spencer barked to Leighton Van Buren on the phone. "I need you to be on, do you understand me? *On.*"

Leighton stood outside a bar named Tap That and took a deep breath, nodding. "Bring it. Right. Got it." Her stomach hurt because she really kind of sucked at bringing it. She could hear her mother yelling, "Sparkle, baby!" as she shoved her onto the stage at beauty pageants. That terror of having no clue at five years old how to sparkle.

She still didn't know how to sparkle. She wasn't even sure what it meant, exactly.

She could organize your spreadsheets.

Be on time.

Create an elaborate party theme.

Corral a pack of barking Chihuahuas.

All of which she had done, and excelled at, as her boss Sadie's Creative Director for the hit bridal show, *Wedding Crashers.*

"I'm trusting you, Leighton. I really, desperately feel like you need to push yourself. I know you're nervous, but you can do this. Our recent footage has just been dull and I have the producer on my ass. I need you to whip this bride up and get some outrageous footage before I get to wherever we're going next week."

"Beaver Bend, Minnesota," Leighton said, her palms starting to sweat as she stood on the sidewalk outside of a classic bar. Like a roadhouse bar. A dive bar. Nothing like what she was used to in Los Angeles. There were no bouncers or doormen or lines to get in the club. Not that she ever went to clubs at home, but she saw them. Here the Tap That sign was fluorescent, glowing in the darkness of a Minnesota summer night. The parking lot was crowded with trucks and motorcycles and what seemed odd to her, minivans. She was expecting a biker gang to burst out at any moment or maybe a Patrick Swayze lookalike to strut out and call her "little lady."

"Oh, that's right, Minnesota. God, why do they send us to these places?" Sadie asked with a groan.

"Everyone loves a small town, Sadie. It's good TV. Most of America is not LA and New York City and people want something relatable. I should go meet up with the bride though. I'll call you tomorrow."

"Fun, Leighton. Give good face, seriously, or we're going to have to talk about your future at *Wedding Crashers*."

Wait. What? She was going to be *fired*? Oh, my God. Leighton didn't even know what she said as she mumbled her way through a goodbye. She could not lose this job. She couldn't. Like, she really couldn't. She had signed a non-compete contract so no one else in LA would hire her in the industry. Which was her only skill set, unfortunately.

On a day-to-day basis she loved this job. Florals and lace and organization made her happy. Her parents were already disappointed in her and if she got fired from the job they had gotten her an interview for, she had no idea what she would do with her life. She was the two things that did not fly in LA—introverted and not a size zero. Not even close. It had been an annoyance her whole life, which was frustrating because she happened to like herself. She was smart, she was thoughtful, she was creative. And she was short and curvy and all one hundred percent natural because she was content with the way she looked.

Her mother and Sadie might beg to differ, but Leighton felt no need to change who she was.

Besides, she was good at this damn position. She was. Why did she have to "bring it?" Which she thought was code for being a person who talked a lot at a high volume. That was Sadie's job. Her responsibility was to do everything else. And side note, she didn't do the casting for these segments. If the bride wasn't excited enough, she wasn't sure how that was her fault, but whatever. There was no use arguing with an egomaniac of a boss.

Dropping her phone into her clutch, she rubbed her palms down the front of her peach cocktail dress. She was fairly certain she had dressed wrong for this venue. Appropriate dress was always her goal and she might have missed the mark this time. But it was the bride-to-be's bachelorette party and she had envisioned dinner and cocktails. That's what the bride had said. Dinner and cocktails.

More like beer and cock.

That was the horrified thought that entered Leighton's mind when she yanked open the heavy wood door and stepped into a crowd of women clapping and cheering for male strippers. She actually heard herself gasp before she quickly pressed her lips together.

Oh, no. This was not her arena. She was Sunday brunches and botanical gardens. Quiet events, where she could fade into the flowers and pretend she didn't have social anxiety. Not loud raucous bars with beer and...booty.

"Holy..." She swallowed hard as she studied the four men on stage in various state of undress, hip thrusting and dancing and winking.

She was used to buff men in LA. They were everywhere,

wearing plunging V-necks and golden tans. But they were polished, high-maintenance, attention seeking. These guys were manly men. Manly, like they legitimately strolled in from their day job and started stripping. They looked real and like they were having a blast, not making a buck.

One was a hockey player. Another was wearing a suit. The third was in a mechanic's work uniform and tool belt.

Then there was the cop.

Leighton swallowed hard as she took in the sight of him. Black pants, shiny black shoes. No shirt, displaying a muscular chest, with a faint farmer's tan. A tan from the sun, not the salon. Handcuffs swirling around his finger, mirrored sunglasses covering his eyes. He had black short hair, tidy and trim. But it was his expression that really did her in. He did not look suave or charming or amused.

He looked like the kind of man who would pick a woman up, throw her against a wall, and make her scream with pleasure.

How she knew that, she had no idea. She'd never been thrown against a wall in her life.

Flustered, Leighton fanned herself and tore her gaze away from the strippers. She needed to find the bride and "bring it," not get a tingle in her vagingle for a total stranger in Beaver Bend. Ironic name, that was. Her beaver would bend over backwards for that cop. There were groups of women of all ages, and a few men. The bartender was shaking his head as he watched the act on stage, like he found the whole thing ridiculous.

Finally, Leighton spotted Winnie Schwartz, the bride who had won a spot on *Wedding Crashers*. The way the show worked was Sadie's team came in, did a whirlwind makeover of the wedding that the bride and groom had planned, then blew on back out. Leighton usually arrived a week in advance to secure a new venue and arrange for floral, catering, etc, while Sadie flew in the day before the actual wedding. Leighton didn't do any filming. It was all presented as if every creative idea and venue hot spot was Sadie's idea, not Leighton's. But because this particular couple did not have a gut-wrenching backstory to film, Sadie wanted Leighton to manufacture some outrageous moments. A crew was meeting her here in twenty minutes to get some clips of the bride with her friends at her bachelorette party. They would film three or four hours so they had plenty of shots and moments to draw from to get about sixty seconds of footage. Surely Leighton could force herself to be witty or adorable or probing and pushy or *something* in that timeframe to force a reaction.

She found herself desperately wishing her mother were here. Barbie Van Buren knew how to make drama happen.

Winnie, having met with her that afternoon, recognized Leighton and stood up. She enthusiastically waved her over.

Yep, Leighton had chosen the wrong outfit. Winnie was in tight jeans and an equally form-hugging T-shirt that read "Cheers, Bitches." There was a veil on her head and a large dildo on a string of beads around her neck. She was going to have to lose the penis before filming. Leighton hated to be a cockblock but they were a so-called family show.

Winnie reached out and enveloped her in a hug when she got to the table. Having come from a family who avoided physical affection like an IRS audit, Leighton was always startled when people she barely knew invaded her personal space. But in the interest of bringing it, she hugged Winnie back. They had clicked when they'd met that afternoon. Winnie had zero social awkwardness and Leighton envied that. She had also thought Winnie seemed genuinely in love with her fiancé and happy with her career as a dog groomer. It must be nice to have everything you'd ever wanted. Or at least confidence in what you said.

Leighton had never had that. She'd developed a stutter by age three and her mother's insistence that beauty pageants would fix the problem had done nothing but erode her already shaky confidence. The stutter had eventually gone away, the anxiety had not. Even as she hugged Winnie back and asked her if she were having fun, she was wishing they could sit down. Standing in the middle of a crowd of seated people made her far too much the center of attention. All she could think was that everyone was looking at her and were probably annoyed that she was blocking their view.

"Sit, sit!" Winnie said, grabbing an empty chair from the next table and pulling it next to her.

It was jutting out into the aisle and blocking the server's path, but at least Leighton could sink down into obscurity. Loud social events just wrung her nerves.

That blissful relief lasted all of one minute before an attractive and fit brunette bounded onto the stage with a mic and shouted, "Let's hear it for our bachelorette party! Congrats to Winnie Schwartz on her upcoming nuptials to Todd Lawrence!"

Winnie gave an ear-splitting shriek of excitement.

The *Wedding Crashers* cameraman, Jackson, appeared at Leighton's side, hunched down so he could talk to her. "It's going to be hard to set anything up in here," he yelled, cupping his hand to her ear. "We don't have any room for lighting or a mic it's so crowded. Do you think we can clear some of these people out?"

Leighton studied the enthusiastic women drinking and having fun. "Uh, no. I'm not throwing these people out of a Friday night hot spot." She envisioned being punched in the face by an irate Minnesotan. "Just get a few shots of Winnie and then we can interview her in the parking lot."

"Come on up here, Winnie," the woman up front with the mic said. "The Tap That Dancers want to congratulate you."

Winnie leapt up with a dexterity that made Leighton's eyes widen. It was like she'd won ten million dollars.

"Come on, girls!" she said to her bridesmaids.

Four women around the table stood up with varying degrees of enthusiasm, but they were all good-natured.

"You, too, Leighton!" Winnie grabbed her arm.

"Oh, no..." She shook her head in horror. "It's your wedding, I couldn't. No, no."

"I insist!" Winnie tugged harder.

Leighton shot a look of panic at Jackson, who had known her for two years.

He grinned. "Go for it."

"Traitor." She had thought he would save her. But he looked amused by the prospect. "I can't do this, Jackson."

"Of course you can." He gave her a double thumbs up. "Have some fun for a change."

Fun. Why couldn't people ever appreciate that her idea of fun did not involve booty grinding? Her fun was a book, a cup of tea, and smelling the roses. Literally. Not dancing on a platform.

But before she could figure out a strategy to hide behind one of the muscled men and give a few tepid dance moves, Winnie shoved her up on stage and she collided with the hockey player. "Oh, my God, I'm sorry," she murmured, feeling her cheeks burn.

"No problem." He tried to move past her and they both went the same way and bumped into each other again. He laughed.

Leighton was horrified. She jumped backward and landed against a wall. Only that wall had arms that reached out and steadied her. Anxiety causing her throat to constrict, she whirled around and found herself face-to-face with the stern and super sexy cop. She had to raise her chin to look into his eyes and what she saw there made her want to die. He wasn't laughing. She opened her mouth to apologize but nothing came out.

It was at that moment one of Winnie's bridesmaids felt compelled to twerk. On Leighton's ass. A strangled gasp emerged from her mouth and she felt sandwiched between a rock and a hard place. Trapped between a jiggly female booty and a very firm, very unrelenting stripper cop, Leighton had no idea where to go or what to do. She felt the telltale rush of heat up her neck and to her temples, the one that said she was about to have a full-blown panic attack.

Her expression must have revealed her distress because the man said, "It's okay. Take a deep breath."

Then he firmly gripped her upper arms and moved her away from the twerking and to the rear of the stage. She tried to speak again but nothing came out. She had no idea what she would say anyway when he wrapped his arm around her lower waist and drew her against him, snug and tight against his chest. Her hands were trapped between her chest and his and she felt the warmth of his bare skin. She really wished he was wearing a shirt. It was too intimate, so she actually shifted her hands to his biceps and looked up at him, wondering what he was doing but too freaked out to really care.

He was a solid, manly anchor, mooring her to the floor in the midst of her crashing waves of anxiety.

"Listen to the music," he said. "Focus on the beat." He moved her hips slowly with his to the pounding bass of the pop song playing.

He had sharp cheekbones that she studied, mesmerized by him. His eyes were a deep rich amber, with flecks of gold around the pupils. Leighton drew a breath in through her nose and tried to relax. The sounds of the room had receded. It was the feel of his hands on her waist, the sway of their bodies together, his confident, take-charge expression that she focused on. It was clear he had seen her panic and he was helping her calm down. It struck her as unbelievably intuitive and kind. She wasn't sure she had ever had a total stranger read her and step in immediately.

Leighton knew the song and she found her voice again, softly singing along with the lyrics to distract herself. This wasn't a song most people would slow dance to, yet she and this man were and it felt right. Easy. Separate from the booty grinding and excited screaming behind her. She was facing him and the wall behind him, not the bar, and she felt the panic recede. She had passed the moment of danger where she might have gone into a full-blown attack.

The song wound down and she pulled back, grateful but ready to get off the stage. "Thank you for that," she said, assuming he would know what she meant. "I'm Leighton."

"Axl. Pleasure to meet you." He didn't smile. But he did release her.

Leighton shivered. Even his name was sexy. "You, too. Seriously, thank you."

Then before she could get roped into staying on stage for another song, she got the hell out there, jumping down the two steps with a speed she hadn't known she was capable of.

Jackson was filming.

"I better not be in that frame," she said as she flung herself into her chair and wished like hell a glass of wine would mysteriously appear in her hand.

"Nice moves," he commented, setting his camera down on the floor beside him. "I've never seen anyone slow dance to Cardi B."

"I'm not discussing this," she said. "Ever."

Jackson snorted. "You know how Sadie likes to give

everyone office nicknames? I think yours is about to be changed to Dancing Queen."

Still flushed, Leighton said in pure exasperation, "Yours is going to be Dickhead."

Given that she rarely swore *or* stood up for herself Jackson was so stunned he just about fell out of his chair laughing.

It actually made the corner of her mouth turn up. The stripper cop had saved her ass, but from Jackson's perspective it must have been bizarre as hell. "I guess I can live with Dancing Queen. It's better than my current nickname."

"Agreed. Amazon Prime is a wonderful thing, but not when your boss is calling you that."

Leighton pulled her phone out, checking to see if she had missed any calls. "No, it's not." Sadie thought it was clever. She liked to say she could get anything from Leighton in two days or less.

Winnie and her friends came back to the table, laughing and reaching for their cocktails. Leighton went back to work, discussing with Jackson how to set up an interview with Winnie.

But she felt eyes on her and she glanced over at the bar.

The stripper cop was watching her.

A shiver rolled up her back and heat pooled between her thighs.

Yum.

That's all she could think. Just yum.

"WHO IS THAT GIRL?" Axl Moore asked his best friend and owner of Tap That, Sullivan O'Toole. "The one I was dancing with."

"I have no idea," Sullivan said. "I've never seen her before." He was behind the bar as usual, serving both customers and himself. He shrugged, like he couldn't care less. Which he probably couldn't.

Sullivan had been no stranger to the bottle since his wife Kendra had died from breast cancer two years earlier at twenty-seven. This was the second year Axl and the other guys from high school had done this entertaining charity strip event in Kendra's memory. Sullivan seemed a little less annoyed by it than he had the previous year when they'd done it, but he still refused to participate in the choreographed, albeit bumbling, routine they did.

"If you don't know her, she must be new in town."

Sullivan knew everyone from being the bar owner.

"She's... different," Axl said. He meant it in a good way. She seemed delicate, like his grandmother's tea set. Look, don't touch. It wasn't that she was waifish. She was actually sporting a true hourglass figure, which he thought was sexy as hell. His hands had felt enormous on her tiny waist and she had been substantially shorter than him, but that full chest had been a thing of beauty. Damn. Axl searched the room for her and found her sitting next to a skinny guy with shaggy hair and glasses. Maybe that was her boyfriend. More her type than he was, probably, not that he was thinking anything in that direction.

Not much, anyway.

She just had him curious. That was all. Not much changed in Beaver Bend. Not many new faces. A new resident was noteworthy. Especially one with an unusual name, wearing a pastel cocktail dress in Tap That.

Lilly, Kendra's best friend, sat down on the stool next to Axl. "Who are we talking about?"

"Leighton. The girl I was dancing with. Who is she?" They hadn't been dancing so much as he had been holding her up. She had been on the verge of a panic attack. He recognized the signs. His best buddy in the marines had endured them frequently after their deployment.

"She's part of the crew for that TV show, *Wedding Crashers*. Winnie won a wedding makeover."

So not a new resident then. He had vaguely heard something about that, but to be honest, weddings didn't interest him, so he'd zoned out on the details. "How long are they in town?"

He shouldn't ask. But he couldn't seem to stop himself. For some reason his mother's text popped into his head. *Maybe you'll meet a nice girl.* Leighton looked like a nice girl. With a body built for sin.

"Until the wedding next Saturday. I imagine they leave on Sunday. Gives you eight plus days." Lilly gave him a sidelong stare. "Got the hots for the California girl, huh? Doesn't seem like your type."

"What is my type?" he asked automatically because he didn't really have one, he didn't think. But what he did know was that girl did not seem like a Hollywood type. She had been genuinely scared to be thrust up on stage in front of everyone. It was classic stage fright.

"Outdoorsy. Athletic."

Axl reflected on that. "Guess I can't argue that." He loved camping, fishing, boating. Anything that allowed him to be outside. He'd always been into nature, even more so now that he'd come home after his enlistment. Walls closed in on him. He needed to see the sky. "So, like you?" he said wryly. Lilly was a guy's girl. Everyone's buddy. She liked to push herself physically and took no shit from anyone. Except Sullivan. She had a soft spot for that idiot.

Lilly cracked up. "Yes. But no. We're like brother and sister. I just see you with a woman who can share your hobbies, that's all."

"I see him with no one," Sullivan said, giving him crap.

"When was the last time you had a girlfriend? Senior year in high school?"

"Last year, dickhead. I'm selective." He let that hang there for a second. It was no secret Sullivan had been less than picky in who he had sex with since Kendra had died. He maintained it wasn't his fault that women came in, drank too much, and wanted to bang, but Axl had known the guy a long time. Since fourth grade. Sullivan was numbing his feelings. Kendra had been his one and only. His first—and what he had thought would be his last—love.

Axl had never had that kind of connection. He had experienced what he would deem nice relationships. Two very pleasant, one a little tumultuous. But not crazy passion or deep, endearing love. Just... nice. A lifelong marriage didn't seem to be in the cards for him, and he knew it was his fault. He struggled to make deep connections with women, and he spent a lot of his life trying to convince his family and friends there was nothing wrong with that. Not much, anyway.

Sullivan gave a snort. "You're boring. That's what you are."

"Guys, guys, knock it off." Lilly eyed Axl. "So are you going to make a move on Cali Girl? If so take her a glass of rosé. It's the in wine right now."

"I thought only my ancient great aunt liked pink wine. That's a thing now?"

Lilly nodded and patted his arm. "It's a thing. I promise. But I don't expect you, the hockey player turned marine turned cop to understand anything that isn't laden in testosterone. Don't worry, I have your back. Pour, Sullivan."

Axl eyed the glass of wine Sullivan handed him dubiously. "Do I trust her?" he asked.

Sullivan shrugged. "I mean, women drink it here. But do Minnesota tastes reflect California? Fuck if I know."

"Nothing ventured, nothing gained. But give me a beer too."

He didn't drink a lot but he was thirsty and a cold beer sounded perfect for the moment. He had put his shirt back on but hadn't bothered to button it up. He took the time to do that now because he felt like a douche going over there flashing chest. That was more their buddy Rick's style, not his.

He went over to the table crowded with women and the lone guy, who Axl realized now had a camera sitting in his lap. He knew nothing about weddings but from the manic excitement on Winnie's face, winning whatever she had won was a huge score. One of the women at the table was Sloane O'Toole, Sullivan's sister. She worked at the groomer's with Winnie. He said hi to her then gestured for her to give up her seat for him. She was in the chair to the left of Leighton.

Sloane raised her eyebrows. "I have no idea what that weird expression you're making means," she said. "And that wine better be for me."

"That's Rick's job to fetch booze for you, not mine." Sloane was two years older than the guys and she had been annoyed by all of them in their growing-up years. They were loud, rough and tumble, and then later, they'd all been a little in awe of Sloane, the hot older cheerleader. But none so much as Rick. It had taken him a dozen years but he'd scored his fantasy girl and they really seemed like an awesome couple now. Axl was happy for both of them. "But I can give you this beer if you want. I haven't even sipped it yet."

She reached her hand out then paused mid-reach. "Wait. What do I have to do in return?"

He leaned over and murmured so only she could hear him. "Give me your seat so I can talk to the TV chick."

"Ah. There's the catch." Sloane looked amused. "Give me the beer." She took the bottle from him and stood up. "For the record, she's not your type."

"I don't have a type." He didn't even date that much. Why

did Sloane and Lilly seem so confident that Leighton was not for him? That was annoying. And good thing the music was pumping some serious bass or she probably would have heard this conversation. "Go find your boyfriend and see what he's got in his tool belt for you."

Sloane laughed loudly. She placed her hand on his arm and squeezed. "Safety first, Axl. Wrap it before you tap it."

His response was a grin. "I'm flattered you think I'm good enough that I'll need to wrap anything tonight."

She gave him an eye roll.

Then she was gone and he was dropping into the chair next to Leighton. He set the glass of wine down in front of her. "You look like you needed a drink."

Leighton turned and stared at him with wide eyes. "I think that seat is taken."

Not quite the response he was hoping for. "Sloane went to find her boyfriend. It's my seat now."

Her mouth opened, but she didn't say anything. For a long heartbeat they just stared at each other while she seemed uncertain how to proceed. She had long, dark eyelashes, at odds with her blonde hair that fluttered as she looked at him. She was beautiful in a quiet way and he took the moment to study her obviously natural and delicate features. Axl had learned how to be still in the military and it didn't bother him to just watch her and wait. She would be too polite to tell him to fuck off.

He was right. She broke their gaze and reached for the wine. "Thank you. I am quite thirsty."

But the cameraman intervened. "Leighton. You shouldn't drink that. You didn't watch the bartender pour it."

For a second Axl was fucking offended. But then he realized the guy had a valid point. They didn't know him or his character. He would give the same advice to his female friends. She looked torn and a little sheepish.

Axl let her off the hook. "Good call, man," he said to the guy. "You never know who is a dirt bag. Here, I'll drink it so you know I'm above board." He lifted the glass and took the wine down in one long swallow. It was like a bowl of sugar exploding in his mouth. He grimaced. "Shit, that's sweet. Oh, my God." His whole face was contorting.

Leighton gave a soft laugh. "Not your drink of choice?"

"Hell, no." He reached past Leighton and held out his hand for the cameraman. "Axl Moore."

"Jackson." He shook his hand.

Then he turned back to Leighton. "If you come up to the bar with me I can get you a drinkable drink."

"Oh, I don't know. That's really sweet, but I have to work. We need to interview Winnie and her friends."

Axl stared at her for a second. He wasn't sure if he was being blown off or not, but in either case, it didn't matter. He wasn't going to get to talk to her. "Understood. Well, it was nice to meet you, Leighton. Maybe I'll see you around town." If the cameraman wasn't sitting there acting like he had no clue Axl was making a play for Leighton, he would have asked for her number.

Leighton nodded. "Maybe. And thank you. For what you did. I appreciate it."

"You're welcome. You're a good dancer."

She smiled. "And you're sweet."

"I can't say sweet would be the word most people use to describe me." But Axl stood up and gave her a head nod. "Enjoy your night."

"You too."

As he walked away he heard the cameraman say, "I'm glad I was here to save your ass. A guy like that? You'll find yourself with your ankles on his shoulders by midnight."

Axl's cock hardened at the thought. Damn right. That had

been the plan he'd already been half formulating without even realizing it.

"Would that be a bad thing?" Leighton asked in a curious and high-pitched voice.

Fuck.

He came to a halt and turned back to them. "No. It wouldn't be a bad thing at all. More like the best way to end your day. And mine."

TWO

SHE GASPED, obviously unaware he'd overheard them. But hey, he had good hearing.

He gave her a dirty, sexy smile and turned back and went to the bar.

The plan was to be there all night. If she wanted to see what a Minnesota man could do in bed, she would find him at some point.

Except that she didn't.

And he went to bed with blue balls and had dirty-ass dreams about the petite blond with the big green eyes and the perfect cupid's bow of a mouth.

A mouth that slid deliciously over his cock while she stared up at him with lustful adoration.

He woke up thinking he had to see Leighton again.

Either that or Sullivan was right and he needed to date more often.

He was working a three to eleven shift, so he got up and went for a run along the lake. He'd purposely chosen his house based on its easy access to the water. It was a bungalow, tucked back in the trees. He would have liked a water view, but even in a small town, that cost a premium. He'd been very conservative with his spending over the years and he decided not to blow that standard by getting a house too rich for his blood. But the water was just down the hill and an easy five-minute jog.

Axl had been like a lot of kids growing up in a small town. He'd wanted to leave, see the world. He had. Then he'd come back. This was home. If he wanted company, he had it. If he didn't, which was frequently, he could be alone. The best of both worlds.

The morning was already heating up. August was guaranteed to be the hottest month of the year and this summer had been particularly brutal. By the two-mile mark he had a sheen of sweat running down his chest and a burn in his calves. He loved it. There was nothing more satisfying than pushing his body. It had been why he'd loved hockey back in his childhood. He hadn't been as fast as Sullivan and Jesse, but he'd had power. Strength.

He peeled his shirt off as he kept running. When he was moving past the picnic area by the beach he realized there was a huge crowd of people gathered around. There were cameras and mics set up. Curious, he turned in and paused at the periphery of the crowd, breathing hard. "What's going on here?" he asked a woman standing there with her middle-school-aged daughters.

"They're filming *Wedding Crashers*," she responded, sounding excited. "Sadie isn't here but they are doing a bunch of interviews and site prep for the wedding next weekend. Lake-front ceremony, I'm guessing."

"Who is Sadie?" he asked, craning to see if he could catch a glimpse of Leighton.

She gasped and looked at him like he was an amoeba. "Sadie Spencer. The host. She's famous. Though I did hear rumors they are looking to replace her with someone younger. Like maybe Sadie Robinson, the daughter from Duck Dynasty. Which honestly, she'd be adorable doing this, don't you think?"

She'd lost him entirely. He didn't even know who she was talking about. "Uh. Sure."

"I mean, a Sadie after a Sadie. It's perfect."

Then he totally lost the thread of conversation because he'd spotted Leighton. She was wearing a pink sundress and giant sunglasses. She had her phone in her hand and she was moving around with authority, talking to the crew and Winnie. She looked confident, completely different from the night before. Being in charge seemed more her element than a bachelorette party.

"Hey, aren't you the cop from Tap That last night?" the woman asked him. She covered her youngest daughter's ears with her palms. "The *stripper?*" she whispered.

Her older daughter gave a crack of laughter. "I thought you went to book club, Mom."

"I did! Then we went to a charity event."

"Uh-huh."

"It really is a charity event," Axl told the daughter. "And ma'am, I'm not a stripper. I'm actually a police officer. We do the dance to honor Kendra O'Toole and raise money for breast cancer research. It's meant to be fun and get some attention."

"You got my attention all right." She eyed him appreciatively.

"Ew," her daughter said. "Mom, stop, seriously, before I need therapy."

That made Axl laugh. "That's a two-way street, kid."

"Listen to the policeman," the woman said, finally dropping her hands from her younger daughter's ears.

"Have a nice day," Axl said. He gave a wave, did a few stretches, and started running again. He went closer to the LA crew just to get a better look at Leighton.

His shirt was tucked in the waistband of his gym shorts. He realized a little too late running shirtless could be perceived as intentional. Showing off.

But Leighton was so wrapped up in studying her phone and consulting with her colleagues that she didn't even notice him.

Damn, there was something so sweet and vulnerable and strong and sexy about her. She seemed like she was very complex. Layered. Intriguing.

It wasn't often he was this curious about a woman. He honestly couldn't remember the last time. Of course, at this point in his life, five years out of the marines, he knew all the single females in Beaver Bend. There were no surprises. A sea of familiar faces.

Then there was this woman. Totally different from his type, according to Lilly and Sloane. But someone he wanted to sit across the table from and talk to. He wanted to hear what she had to say, because he had a feeling she wasn't a flirt. She would say whatever she meant. Like him.

Okay, and he wanted to take her to bed and fuck her. There was that. He definitely couldn't shake the image of her ankles on his shoulders thanks to that cameraman. She had a very *juicy* figure. The kind you slap and tickle and bite.

And pound.

Axl cleared his throat. Yeah. He needed to get laid. That was clear.

But there was no reason for him to hang around when she wasn't glancing his way at all, so Axl returned to his run.

Thirty minutes later he was home, in a cold shower.

No Cali girl for him, not even for a few days. He wasn't going to be an asshole and track her down.

TWO HOURS after that he was doing basic patrol when a red

sedan with Illinois plates flew past him doing way over the speed limit.

He threw on his lights and pulled the car over in a routine traffic stop.

But when he came up to the window and opened his mouth, he was shocked to see Leighton behind the wheel, looking at him in exasperation. He found himself pleased that she was a little speed demon. It gave him another opportunity to talk to her.

"Hi, Leighton," he said. "Are you aware you were going twenty miles over the speed limit?"

"Oh, I get it," she said, staring up at him, hands raking her wavy hair back off her face. "Is there where you tell me you're giving me a ticket for being sexy or something canned like that?"

It wasn't often that Axl found himself speechless. Or so thoroughly confused. But completely amused. "Excuse me? You were speeding. I need to see your driver's license. I'm guessing this is a rental car, so if you have the rental agreement I'd like to see that too, please."

Axl bent down and swept his eyes over the vehicle. There was nothing noteworthy. Just Leighton's purse on the passenger seat and her phone in the cup holder. There was a camera on the dash, which struck him as odd, but maybe it was for filming bits for the wedding show. He had no clue how those shows worked.

Leighton shot him a look he couldn't decipher. "What if I say no? Does that mean you'll have to pat me down? Hopefully?"

He glanced at the camera again. Was he on TV, being punked? Or was Leighton just nuts? Because she looked a little glassy-eyed, to be honest, and sounded nothing like she had the night before. "I need to see your driver's license."

. . .

LEIGHTON TRIED to channel bringing it. What would bringing it entail in this circumstance?

Flirting. Sexual innuendo. Being brazen and bold.

She took a deep breath and reminded herself how much she loved her job and how high her rent was. If this was a test from Sadie, having her fake pulled over by a stripper cop, she had to pass it. Play along.

"You're really sticking to character. I admire that. Big, tough cop. Picture of authority." She reached for her purse and pulled out her wallet. She produced her license with a smile and an exaggerated wink. "Here you go, Officer Hottie."

Just saying that almost killed her. She felt *ridiculous*.

Axl didn't look like he was buying it either. He looked dubious at best.

"Leighton Van Buren. Age twenty-six. Beverly Hills. You live in Beverly Hills?" he asked, sounding surprised.

Why did he sound so stunned? She had been raised in Beverly Hills. It wasn't like she'd bought a fake ID on the internet. So typical. Everyone always wanted her to be someone or something she wasn't.

"I was living with my parents when I got this license. I have my own apartment now in Silver Lake." Now she was oversharing for no reason. Awkward.

"I'm going to go run your license. I'll be right back."

She panicked. She'd gotten distracted. She wasn't flirting or getting good footage. There was a dashcam in her rental car and for all she knew, Sadie was sitting back in the office scoring her live.

"Is that when you ask me to spread 'em?" Leighton winked at him a second time. Or attempted to wink. It was more of an exaggerated squint this time. Her voice sounded more manic than flirtatious.

Axl eyed her. Not with interest, but wariness. "Leighton, I need you to step out of the car."

She hid a wince. Dang it. This was a full-on disaster. Closing her eyes for one brief second, she imagined what her best friend, Zach, would say in these circumstances. Zach was sassy and confident and a wicked flirt.

"It's about time." She opened the door and rose to her full height, which wasn't much. She barely came up to his shoulders. God, he was really sexy. Just so broad and manly and stern. It made her heart rate increase and her nipples start to firm beneath her sundress.

She held her wrists out to him. "Are you going to cuff me for being naughty?" she asked, going for seductive. "Do I have to bribe my way out of this?"

His eyebrows shot up. "Have you been drinking? Or taking prescription drugs?"

If someone had written a script for him, they should be fired. What a dumb line. There was nothing sexy about narcotics. "Of course not! It's two in the afternoon."

"I'm going to need you to take a breathalyzer. Do you know what that is?"

Ah, here it was. A blow job joke. "Sure. Just tell me where to *blow*." Her gaze dropped down to his crotch.

"I need you to come and get in the car, Leighton."

This wasn't going the way Leighton had expected. She was flirting as hard as she could with Axl and he didn't seem to be getting it. Maybe Sadie had paid him to stay in character to a certain point.

But this was way harder than she had imagined. Wasn't it a stripper's job to make the "customer" happy? Her own job was on the line and she was blowing it. Or *not* blowing it, apparently, since he hadn't reacted positively to her innuendo. Or wait, had he? Is that why he wanted her to get in his car?

Oh, hell no. No matter how much she needed this job and no matter how good looking Axl was, the thought alone made her sweat. She didn't give blowjobs on the side of the road to anyone. Actually, it had never come up in her life before but it just figured that somehow her flirting sucked so hard he thought she wanted to suck hard.

Disaster. She was a total disaster.

But she needed Sadie to think she was going along with this whole fake cop stripper pulling her over.

It was the game. Part of "bringing it."

Sadie had been quite clear again this morning on what she needed to do. She had specifically said that today there would be a test. A big test she needed to pass. That Leighton had to be bubbly and flirty and fun. Always the f word.

That damn f word.

Not to mention sparkle. And now bringing it. All phrases that could die, because they were vague and subjective.

If this wasn't the test, she had no idea what would be. This had Sadie written all over it. Pulled over by a cop. Please. She hadn't been driving that fast.

But now she was freaked out because if he whipped it out in his patrol car she would faint. Plus, Axl wanted to take her out of camera range. She had a dashboard cam that was meant for Winnie to record a video diary about the *Wedding Crashers* process and her expectations for her wedding but once Leighton had seen Axl come to the window, she had turned it on. Proof that she got the joke and could roll with it.

So, she had to stay in range. "Um, I don't think so." She tried to lean back against her car artfully, but she partially fell into the open window. Righting herself, she laughed and fluttered her eyelashes at him. "Whoops."

"I need you to come with me, miss."

He sounded very stern. "Oh, you are so serious." For a

stripper he was a good actor. She'd give him that. It was very difficult for her not to be obedient. It was just her personality to follow directions.

But she had to stay strong. Her future at *Wedding Crashers* rested on it. She stayed put, trying to strike a sexy pose against the car.

"I need you to walk a straight line for me from your car to my patrol car. Stay away from the road."

If she walked over there she could just walk back and be in camera range again so that Sadie could see she was fun and flirty. It seemed like her best bet. So she did, fast-walking in a straight line and immediately returning. "Done."

He flashed a light in her eyes.

"What the heck?" she asked, pupils dilating. "That kind of hurts."

"I need you to hand me your purse. What prescription drugs do you take on a daily basis?"

Leighton frowned. "None." Well, birth control, but that was none of his business. She was starting to think something was wrong here. "Where did you get an actual patrol car from? That's very impressive." That must have cost a ton of money. She had witnessed Sadie go to great lengths to create elaborate pranks on staff members but this seemed extreme even for her.

A niggle of concern started to rise in Leighton.

Maybe Sadie would fire her before she went to these elaborate lengths. This was an elaborate scheme, even for a TV host with a full crew at her disposal. Now she was full of doubt about everything.

"Okay. You're coming with me."

Axl grabbed her arm and she had to admit she felt a shiver that had nothing to do with concern. His strong grip was arousing. But then he whirled her around and slapped handcuffs on her left wrist.

"What—"

So she had joked about spreading them. She hadn't actually meant it. They weren't in a club at a strip show. This was the side of the road.

Her other wrist went into the cuffs.

Her concern increased dramatically.

"Just stand still. I'm patting you down then I'm putting you in the car to run your license."

This felt a little too real. Leighton swallowed hard and leaned against her car. She gave a startled squawk when he spread her legs. "Um, what is going on?"

She was torn between feeling a little aroused by how hot Axl was and how he was running his hands over her calves, and at the same time feeling like: one, something was off, and two, she could not let a total stranger dive under her dress even if it was part of his script.

It wasn't a particularly comfortable position with her hands behind her back and her body off-balance, relying on her rental car to hold her up. Axl's hands were rising higher and higher and she grew seriously alarmed. When he touched her inner thighs just above the knee she jumped.

And tried to move away. She wasn't sure if he was intending to go any further but she wasn't sticking around to find out. Leighton jerked her body to the left, slamming into the mirror and wincing, stumbling backwards.

Suddenly without warning, she lost her balance and without her hands to right herself, she went down hard, right on her butt. It hurt. Like, a lot. "Ow." She sat there stunned, hair in her face, dress up over her thighs, hands cuffed behind her back. "Okay, I admit it. Sadie wins. This isn't fun. I'm not fun. F the f word. Maybe I am not cut out for this."

"Are you okay?" Axl asked, bending over.

She nodded. "I think so." She was going to have a hell of a bruise on her ass, but she would live.

"I'm going to touch you to help you up, okay?"

He was talking to her like she might spook if he laid a finger on her.

That's when she heard the radio in his car crackle and a very official sounding voice come on mentioning codes and something about a patrol car needed downtown.

Leighton frowned. She had a horrible sinking feeling. "Wait a minute. Are you a *real* cop?"

Axl hauled her to her feet in front of her car. "What do you mean? Of course I'm a real cop. These don't give these cars, a badge, and a gun to just anyone who asks for one." He was eyeing her like she was insane or an idiot.

She wasn't certifiable but she still felt pretty stupid. "I thought you were a stripper," she said. "You were stripping last night," she added, in case he had stumbled up on stage during an amnesia episode.

But now that she blew her hair out of her face and studied him from head to toe, he did look very legit. He had a gun. He had very shiny shoes. And a uniform that had an official-looking insignia. His hat had a patrolman's number on it. She swallowed the enormous lump that had started crawling up her throat.

Well.

This could be bad.

"It was a charity event," he said. "For breast cancer awareness. The owner of the bar, he and I and the other guys go way back, to grade school. Sullivan lost his wife to breast cancer two years ago so this is the second annual 'Tap That' charity event." He did the actual air quotes.

She couldn't see his eyes behind his sunglasses but the corner of his mouth turned up. "I don't use my official uniform on stage and it's a small town. It's like when cops do lip sync videos. It's meant to foster a sense of community."

"Naked chests can do that," she said, in all seriousness. That was certainly true in LA.

Axl laughed. "So, Leighton Van Buren, from Beverly Hills, what in the actual hell did you think was happening here if you didn't think I was a real police officer?"

That was a good question. And an embarrassing one. Her throat started to close. She grabbed at her chest, massaging her skin and rolling her shoulders to try to relax. "I thought my boss set me up. She said I need to be more spontaneous. More fun. So I thought she was monitoring me on the dash cam and that if I wasn't flirty she would be upset with me and fire me." For a second she got lightheaded but she fought the sensation. "I was trying to bring it. You know. Create a moment. Manufacture a reaction." Now she was babbling and she forced herself to stop talking.

For a second Axl didn't say anything. Then he dragged his hand over his mouth, his jaw working. He reached up and removed his sunglasses. There was amusement in his eyes.

Thank goodness. She may still be arrested for harassing an officer, but hopefully he would go easy on her. Her palms were clammy.

"Leighton. I'm actually speechless. That's the most... interesting attempt to get out of a ticket I've ever heard." He tucked his glasses in his shirt pocket. "Can I assume then that you are not on drugs, legal or illegal, or alcohol?"

"Yes. You can assume that."

"I'm still going to run your license." He held his hand up. "You behave yourself. No more sexual innuendos while I'm on duty. Save them for later." He capped that off with a wink to indicate he was teasing her.

Nonetheless, her cheeks were on fire. She wanted to dig a

hole in the asphalt and bury her head in it. "I think my flirting skills are subpar."

"Your flirting skills are just fine. I was debating if I was going to have to arrest you for attempting to bribe a police officer with sex though."

"Holy crap," she blurted out. "That would have been bad. Really bad. Like so bad." She would die. Actually die. She pictured her parents getting that phone call from Sadie. "That is not what I meant, you know."

Leighton offered to blow a cop to get out of a ticket.

Her father would have a heart attack. Given that he was seventy-five, it wasn't that improbable.

Her mother might actually be proud of her though. Barbie Van Buren had long lamented that Leighton couldn't cut loose.

Axl shook his head, like he couldn't believe any of this. "I don't know anything about what the hell is going on here. Turn around and I'll release you."

Obediently, she turned around. He unlocked the handcuffs.

"For the record, if you're telling me the truth, your boss sounds like a piece of work. Why do you have to be flirty to work on a wedding show?"

"I swear I am telling you the truth. I don't have to be flirty, per se, just bubbly. Lively. Interesting. I'm none of those things."

Obviously. If she was, Axl wouldn't be eyeing her like she was bonkers.

Axl clearly didn't think she was fun so much as certifiable.

AXL STUDIED the woman in front of him. He didn't know what to make of her or this situation. It was kind of funny. But it was also kind of awful. So, what, she had to be a performing monkey just to work on a TV show? According to what he'd been told, she wasn't even the host. "What is your job, specifically?"

"I'm the creative director."

"Then why do you have to be bubbly? I'm sorry, I'm still not getting the connection."

"Because I interact with clients. She thinks I don't bring enough energy and whip them up properly. My skills lie more with organization."

"I don't know anything about Hollywood or TV or reality shows or whatever. But what I do know is that you are actually one of the most interesting women I've met in a long time. If I were you, I'd be looking for a new job."

He meant that. She was very interesting. And it seemed like she was completely in the wrong career. But that wasn't really any of his business.

She confirmed that by looking away, down to her feet. When she looked back up again, she looked troubled. She took a few deep breaths. "I need to get to an appointment. Can I just have the ticket for speeding? Since apparently, that's why you actually pulled me over."

Axl wished he was off-duty because he would pick her up, give her a panty-melting kiss, and let her boss figure that shit out. He felt equal parts protective and turned on by her. It wasn't a combination he'd ever really experienced before and he didn't know what to do with it.

"I have to put you in my car." Misunderstanding or not, there was protocol. "I'll be as fast as I can."

She didn't respond, just let him lead her to the patrol car and put her in the back. She looked dejected. He wasn't sure what to make of any of this nonsense. It was a first in his career on the force that someone had thought he was a fake cop. A stripper. Damn, he was torn between never wanting to the guys to find this out ever and just telling them and taking the heat because it was so fucking insane.

And hell, not to brag, but it didn't suck having someone think he looked good without his shirt on.

"You okay?" he asked her, glancing into the back seat as he ran her license. She was biting her lip and looking worried.

"Am I in trouble?"

"No, you're not in trouble." Her license came back clean. He debated even writing the ticket but he decided to do it just because she had recorded the whole damn thing. If that shit went out into the world, he wanted his ass covered that he had followed the book. "You're free to go. I'm going to come around and let you out."

"Thanks, Axl. I mean sir. Officer."

He gave her a grin. "Officer Hottie to you."

She gave a groan and put her hand over her face. "Did I really say that?"

"Oh, you said it." He would never forget it.

"It was an honest mistake."

He wasn't sure that it really was but maybe things were different in her world. "I'm flattered."

Axl stepped out of the car and opened the back door for her. "Slow down. Especially since you're not familiar with these roads." He handed her the ticket. "You can pay this online."

"I don't think I was actually speeding. Are you sure you want to give this to me?" She looked hopeful.

And adorable, but he needed to cover his ass.

"Flattery will only get you so far." He gave her a grin. "Sorry, I have a job to do. Just like you. But let me make it up to you by taking you out for a drink sometime."

Leighton rose from the seat and skirted past him, biting her sensuous full lip and looking indecisive. She really adorable. Axl liked a woman with curves and Leighton had them in all the right spots. She eyed him over her shoulder as she started walking to her car. "You're determined to get me drunk, aren't you? That's twice you've offered me a cocktail."

Now that was real flirting. Natural and sweet and sensual, as opposed to that over-the-top winking and suggestive comments. This suited Leighton much better. He wondered if she even realized she was doing it.

But if she was going to flirt, hell, so was he. "Then maybe you should say yes and accept your fate. And if one cocktail gets you drunk, you're a cheap date."

Leighton cocked her head. "Maybe you should tell me why you want to go out with me. Five minutes ago you thought I was high or a lunatic or both."

Why did he want to go out with her? That was the easiest question he'd ever been asked.

"Because you're gorgeous, for one."

She scoffed, as if she didn't believe him. "Uh, thank you."

Her apparent skepticism actually astonished him but he wasn't going to stand there and argue with her. "I want to get to know you. I find you very interesting."

"You're crazy. I just told you I'm not any fun. Besides, I'm only here a few days."

"What kind of dates do you have in LA that you need more than a few days for them?" he teased her, giving her a sly smile.

Leighton gave a soft laugh, finally dropping the hand she had been holding up to her chest like a shield between them. "I concede the point. But you're still crazy."

"I'm not normally crazy. At all. I'm just decisive. But for the record, interesting isn't a synonym for fun. I don't need to spend time with someone *fun*. I'm not exactly a fun guy myself." He wasn't what anyone would call impulsive either. So, he really couldn't say why at that moment he chose to do what he did.

Other than he wanted to, so he did it. Decisive.

There was something about Leighton. Something about the way she looked so anxious yet determined. Something about the way she could actually think she was average when she had a banging body, full lips, and hair he wanted to wrap his fingers around and tug. Leighton's ass the night before in her tight cocktail dress had brought to mind bringing the palm of his hand down on that delicious flesh and driving them both crazy. "Not everyone wants to get loud and party. Some men like simpler pursuits."

Like kissing. And sex.

"And what would those be?" she asked.

As Leighton reached her car, he leaned down and stared into her green eyes. He let the moment linger, the anticipation hover. "This."

She knew what he was thinking because her eyes widened and her plump lips parted.

It was all the invitation he needed.

Axl bent down and kissed her sensuous mouth. His hand slipped into her blond waves and rested gently at the back of her neck, in case she tried to escape. He just wanted one kiss.

That's what it started as. A simple brush of his lips over hers.

She gave a little gasp, which he swallowed, as he shifted his leg so that he was touching hers. For a second she seemed to hesitate, but then she tentatively gave in and kissed him back with a soft, shy acceptance.

Axl could have quit there. He meant to. But then he took the kiss deeper, just briefly, intending to pull away right after. Then something happened. Leighton sighed into his touch, and she leaned toward him, her full chest pressing against him. Her arms snaked around his waist and she parted her lips in a sweet, dangerous invitation.

When his tongue dipped between those luscious lips and

teased at the tip of her tongue, Axl got hard. So hard so fast that he knew he was in danger of taking this way too far on the side of the road. In his uniform. On-duty.

Holy shit.

He broke off the kiss and stepped back.

She blinked up at him. Her eyes were glassy again, but not from panic. From arousal. Her breath was quick and shallow, causing her substantial chest to rise and fall rapidly. Her cheeks were stained pink, presumably from desire but most likely also embarrassment.

"Meet me for a drink tomorrow," he said. "I can't tonight, I work until eleven, but I want to see you."

She took a deep shuddering breath.

"I'm so confused right now," she said.

"That makes two of us." He stepped back and opened her car door. "I'll call you tomorrow and maybe we can figure this out." With his lips on hers again in private.

She slipped into the driver's seat and nodded, looking dazed. "Right. Okay."

He gave her a smile. As she reached for her seatbelt, he saw the dashcam light blinking. Fuck. "Is that recording?"

She shook her head. "No."

Thank God. "Oh, good, geez, you scared me there."

"It's actually a live feed."

Well, hell. That was a whole lot fucking worse.

He'd just kissed a woman during a routine traffic stop live on the damn Internet.

THREE

LEIGHTON BLINKED AT WINNIE SCHWARTZ, who was in tears.

"What do you mean you don't want to do the show, Winnie? I'm sorry I was late. I got pulled over by a cop who took forever." Because she had propositioned him and he had been kissing her.

Her cheeks heated. She felt guilty and off-kilter, though she hadn't done anything wrong. Not exactly. But she felt like Winnie was staring at her knowing that Leighton had kissed the stripper cop. The *real* cop. The hot cop.

"It's not because you're late. Though I think that gave Todd a few more minutes to cement his decision. He doesn't want to be on TV. He says our wedding isn't a circus. That it's private, not an invitation to be trolled by haters."

She couldn't really argue with that. They were outside an ice cream shop shaped like a gigantic soft serve cone. Winnie's fiancé had left, which was a dick move in Leighton's opinion. He didn't want to do the show? He could be man enough to stay and tell her, not let Winnie deal with it. "I'm sorry he feels that way. Are you sure he isn't just having cold feet about the cameras? Maybe he'll change his mind."

Leighton's palms were damp and she rested them in her lap, trying not to panic. The show's producer would be pissed if they had wasted this trip to Minnesota and she would have to scramble to find a replacement couple in five days. Most likely they would lose next weekend for shooting and would have to push out to the following week, which would throw off their production schedule. All in all, a disaster.

This was so the total opposite of what Sadie had commanded her to achieve.

She was supposed to create a dramatic moment, not kill the show.

"Can I just talk to Todd?" she asked Winnie. She would beg him to do the show.

"No. He is seriously done. It's not happening." Winnie licked a twist cone and used her free hand to wipe her tears. "I really wanted to do this. I mean, we don't have a huge budget. I'm sure whatever you and the show were going to do would be amazing."

Leighton was torn between sympathy and wanting to dangle a carrot. Ultimately, she was too nice to try to twist the screws on Winnie. This was her wedding and it was hugely important to Winnie, obviously. "Everything you had planned is still in place. Nothing has been canceled because that's not how we operate. We pay the original vendors in full when we make our changes so that they don't lose their profit. You can still have the wedding you had planned before you ever even applied to the show."

"Yeah. A lame one."

"Hey, Winnie, it's okay." Leighton had a pit in her gut but she did not want Winnie to be disappointed in her day. "You have to think of your fiancé. What good is an over-the-top wedding if he's totally uncomfortable? The day becomes about the cameras then instead of *you*. It should be about the two of you. About starting a life together."

Winnie sniffled and took another lick. She was wearing full makeup and had done her hair since they were supposed to be filming the couple's requests for the *Wedding Crashers* wedding. "I get it." She sighed. "But I wanted both. I guess that makes me greedy."

"It makes you a girl. Who doesn't want an amazing fairytale wedding?" Leighton reached out and squeezed her arm. "But it will still be amazing."

"Thanks, Leighton. You're a pretty cool chick, you know that? Are you married? I can't believe I didn't ask you that before now. God, I guess I've been kind of self-absorbed."

"I'm not married. I'm single." Mostly always single. She was not about to date an aspiring actor/musician/model. Her last meaningful relationship had been with the guy who made her coffee every morning. That itself was meaningful enough to her but he had asked her out and they'd dated for six months before he had moved back to Iowa. He'd been a sweet enough guy, a little shy, and it had been a nice few months. But she hadn't even thought about marrying him.

Winnie's eyes lit up. "We should set you up with someone here."

Axl Moore popped into her head. That kiss. What the heck had that been about?

She had basically melted against his hard chest, her thoughts scattered and confused. It had been a delicious kiss. Solid, easy, teasing, arousing. She glanced back to the window where the teen girls were working behind the counter making cones. She really wanted one suddenly.

She needed to cool down.

"No, that's okay. Thanks, but that's not a great idea. I'm only here a week."

Winnie eyed her. "Are you blushing? Or are you just hot? It's humid today."

"It's the humidity. We don't have it like this in California." That was true. But it was not the weather causing her to heat up from the inside out.

Winnie picked up her phone, her tears dried up. "I should text Todd and let him know everything is okay." But then she studied her screen. "What is this?" She tapped her screen. "Leighton, are you *making out* with Axl Moore?"

Her stomach dropped. "What?" Sure, the feed had been live, but it went to the staff at *Wedding Crashers*, not out into the world. She didn't think. It never had before. It was meant to capture clips for editing into the show. "What are you talking about?"

Winnie turned her phone. "That *is* you. That is the dress you're wearing right now!"

It was bizarre to see herself on camera. She was leaning against the car, which was unfortunate because she was taking up the majority of the screen. Axl towered over her, and his left arm was clearly visible, a lot of biceps on display. His hand was buried in her hair and yep, they were making out. She swallowed. It looked as good as it had felt.

"Well. Yes. That is me. And Axl." She wasn't sure what else to say beyond that. There was no denying it. She studied Axl. Damn, he was sexy. That dark hair, those strong cheekbones. All those muscles. That massive height. "I need an ice cream cone."

She swung her leg over the picnic table they were seated at and was about to stand up when her phone rang. It was Sadie. Dang it. Terrified, she answered the call. "Hello?"

"What is going on in Minnesota? Jill just got a call from the fiancé who said he is not doing the show."

"I'm on the call too," Jill, the show's producer, said. "Leighton, this is not good. We need to regroup and find someone else in Beaver Bend who wants to take the spot."

"Jill, this is a very small town. I doubt we can find someone."

"Work on it. Ask around. Also, we need to discuss you being clearly more focused on your personal life than your job. I didn't send you to Minnesota to have sex with a police officer."

Oh, God. Leighton hung her head and rubbed her forehead. There was no point in protesting. "Got it." She wanted to ask what glitch had set that clip out into the world but there was no way asking would make it better. *Hey, I thought only my co-workers would see me kissing a cop* didn't sound all that professional.

"I said be more fun, not act like a college girl on spring break," Sadie said.

That seemed like a hell of a leap, but Leighton wasn't going to argue. She was on thin ice. Plus, she was flat-out mortified.

"Find a replacement bride," Jill said. "Or I'm terminating your employment with *Wedding Crashers*."

There it was. Boom. The other shoe dropping. She felt sick and a little lightheaded. "I understand. I'm on it."

She ended the call and took a deep breath. She could feel anxiety crawling over her skin, threatening to squeeze and crush her. Just breathe. There was a solution to every problem.

"Do you have any girlfriends who are engaged and want to get married next weekend?" Leighton asked Winnie.

She shook her head. "No. And if one of my friends took my spot on *Wedding Crashers*, I would cut a bitch. Just saying."

Leighton hadn't even considered that, but she didn't blame Winnie. She'd feel the same way. "Fair enough. I'll just post on social media."

Winnie raised her eyebrows but she didn't question it. "Let me go buy you an ice cream cone. You look like you need it."

Leighton needed the ice cream cone, a Minnesota bride, and a backbone.

Not necessarily in that order.

AXL SAT across from the chief as still as possible. Another lesson he had learned in the military. Just sit silent and don't fidget while you're getting your ass handed to you on a platter. Anything you try to say can and will be used against you.

"You think traffic stops are your personal Tinder? What the fuck, Moore?" The chief was in his fifties, in decent shape, but getting thick around the middle. He had been shaving his head for the entirety of Axl's tenure in the department. He had a wife he adored and three kids not much younger than Axl. He was a fair man, but no-bullshit.

This was the first time he could recall getting ripped a new one by Chief Darcy. It wasn't pleasant, but the Marines had been worse. So he would just take it.

"This is not like you at all. I've never seen you act with anything other than professionalism. Is something going on I should know about?"

That didn't sound good. "No. What do you mean?"

"Are you having some kind of personal crisis? Do we need to see about getting you to a counselor?"

Oh, fabulous. His boss thought he was losing his shit. Add him to the list of people who thought he was "struggling" just because he didn't want to settle down. Though in this case, the chief had a good point. It wasn't like him to do something so unprofessional.

"No, no, seriously. No counselor. It was a lapse in judgment, nothing more. I swear."

"I'm going to have to write you up formally. That video is fucking everywhere."

Axl sat up straighter. That was something he did not want. "What? Seriously?"

The chief stared him down. "If you could tell me she was your girlfriend or something that would be different. But everyone is telling me she's with that TV show that's in town."

There was no time to think. Darcy had given him an out and he was taking it. "What if I told you she *is* my girlfriend?"

"I would say that is a very good thing. But tell me how you met. And make it believable."

Axl had known his boss long enough to know what he was really saying. *Get your fucking story straight.* That's what he was saying.

"We met online," he lied, shocked at how smooth it rolled off of his lips. "She purposely chose a wedding here so we could spend time together."

Darcy gave a snort. "You're full of crap. But I'd better see some wining and dining going on with this girl so that I get to the point where I do believe it."

"Yes, sir." He was going to have to not only wine and dine her but warn her that he was making shit up about her.

His mom reprimanding him for lying as a kid popped into his head. A tangled web and all that. But he just couldn't stomach the idea of being officially reprimanded for kissing Leighton. He wasn't even sure why he had done it.

He just knew that something was tugging at him when it came to her. He had wanted to taste her and he had.

Now he just wanted more.

He wanted her ankles on his shoulders and his cock buried deep inside her softness.

He coughed into his hand.

"Why do I feel like your thoughts are in the gutter right

now?" Chief Darcy threw his phone down on his desk and leaned back into his swivel chair. "This is why celibacy is dangerous, kid. It makes you do stupid shit."

"I can't argue with you there." Being distracted by dirty thoughts wasn't usually a weakness of his, but Leighton was different.

When he had been a kid he had been into rock collecting. He'd dug through dirt, mud, water. He liked to find ones that were different. That had something unique about them. He studied them, polished them, saved them in his dresser drawer.

Leighton had piqued his interest because she was unique. Layered and complex. He wanted to run his hands over her and explore every inch of her skin. It was like he was just cruising through his life and then wham. There was a gem staring at him across the stage at Tap That.

It was totally out of character for him but he was in it now. He had to ride this out and if he was going to catch flak for it he damn well wanted a date with Leighton.

"Maybe you need to think about getting a girlfriend for real."

Axl tried not to sigh. Everyone wanted him in a relationship because apparently, he wasn't normal if he wanted to be single. "Yes, sir."

"Get out of here."

"Yes, sir."

When he left the chief's office he pulled his phone out. The guys were blowing his phone up in a group text.

DUDE.

WTF. Did you take a blow to the head? So not your style, man.

The Cali girl? Nice. Your mom. She was right. Haha.

He wasn't even sure what to say so he settled for a general *Fuck off.* That was enough explanation for right now.

Jesse sent him a gif of a guy making a jerking off motion. *Now you don't have to be this guy for a change.*

Sullivan sent him a picture of a man on his knees being whipped by a dominatrix.

He couldn't even get mad at them. He had done this to himself. Now he had to extract himself from it. He waved to the receptionist who shook her head at him and another patrolman who made mock kissing sounds in his direction. "Yeah, yeah, get it out of your systems."

"Oh, no, we're driving this into the ground," Jack Turner said. They were a similar age and Jack was a perpetual prankster.

"Awesome. Can't wait."

"The Ice Man melts. This is *gold.*"

He hated that stupid nickname. Ice Man. Why, because he didn't talk just to hear himself talk? Because everything wasn't a big fucking joke to him? Because he didn't need all eyes on him at every moment?

Without responding to Jack, he started for the front door.

"Hey, Axl, wait," Susan, the receptionist said. "You have a message from one Leighton Van Buren, who I think you know fairly well." She made a face. "Is that a real name? Anyway, she wants you to call her. She left a number."

Axl stopped in his tracks. He turned around and held his hand out for the slip Susan had been holding. "Thanks."

"You're welcome, Officer Hottie."

Great. So that had been shared too? There was no way the chief was going to believe his story about her being his girlfriend if he watched the whole encounter. He didn't think. Then again, he had approached the car and used her name. He clearly knew her. Plus she had acted flirty. But he hadn't responded the way a boyfriend would.

Damn it. What a mess.

He didn't say anything in return to Susan and she started laughing. Actually, cackling. "This is what happens when you start stripping. Women are throwing themselves at you."

"I bet you want me, too, then, Susan. I saw you at Tap That last night."

Her smile fell off her face. "Jim knows I was there. It's for charity."

"Exactly." He gave her a wink. "See you later."

She looked flustered.

Leaving the building, he was determined to not be bothered by anyone razzing him. But he did not want to be written up. He could take heat. He could take the joke going on for months. But he had aspirations. He wanted to make detective. He did not want to be written up over something so innocent.

Well. Innocent wasn't the right word.

But it wasn't like he had fucked up his job. Or put anyone in harm's way. Or taken a bribe.

Sliding into his squad car, he was about to call the number on the paper when his saw his mother was calling him.

"Shit." If he didn't answer it, she would just keep calling. Time to just take it like a man. "Hello?"

"Can you explain to your mother why you are kissing a woman on the internet?"

He fought the urge to sigh. "Because I didn't know the camera was running."

"This is very erratic behavior, Axl. I know you've been struggling since your discharge but maybe you need to talk to someone."

Now he did sigh. He could never wrap his head around why his mother couldn't just accept that he was a loner. He had not been struggling. Jesus. She worried endlessly about him, which worried him. "Mom. It's fine. Leighton and I know each other."

"I suppose that's reassuring on some level. But unless you're engaged to be married, not really."

Shit. She reached right for the hard stuff. "Mom, I have to go. I'm at work."

"Call me later," she demanded.

"I will." And tell her what, he had no idea. He had inadvertently turned up the heat on himself. His mother already thought he was a head case.

He called the number on the paper Susan had given him. Leighton answered immediately.

"This is Leighton Van Buren."

"Hi, this is Axl. Look, I'm really sorry—"

She cut him off. "Axl, I need your help. Please. Do you know anyone who would want to get married next Saturday? Winnie's fiancé canceled and if I don't find a replacement I'm going to get fired. My producer straight up told me that."

He was momentarily taken aback. He had thought she'd be calling about the kiss but clearly that was not first and foremost in her mind. That was a little insulting, he wasn't going to lie.

"Uh... no. I can't say that I do. Rick and Sloane aren't even engaged yet and none of my other friends are dating anyone." Brandon was living it up in Chicago as a party boy businessman and Jesse was getting ass left right and center on the road as a pro hockey player. Marriage was not on his mind.

Then there was Sullivan. He doubted Sullivan would ever get married again. Not after losing Kendra so young.

"Dang it. This is not good. They saw the video of us too, by the way."

"Who is they?"

Leighton had a smooth feminine voice but now it sounded high-pitched and a little frantic. "Everyone!"

"I'm sorry about that. It was impulsive." He didn't regret it, despite the heat he was taking. Of course, he said that now. If that went on record he might, no matter how sweet and delicious Leighton was.

"I should have pulled away," she wailed. "I didn't stop you at all. I *liked* it." She sounded scandalized by that.

The fact that she liked it mattered more than it should. "Kissing is fun. You wanted to be fun. I don't see what the problem is." He didn't. Not for her. What did her boss care if she was rubbing bodies with a small-town cop? Though he supposed she was probably being paid for her time in Beaver Bend. That might annoy the powers-that-be that she had been briefly unprofessional.

"I don't think anyone particularly cares that we were, you know," she said. "They care more about wasting resources by being here in Minnesota and not being able to film an episode. And they think I'm distracted and Todd canceling is my fault because I didn't massage his concerns enough. That I was too busy having some full-blown love affair."

"It was one kiss," he protested. "Though I have to tell you, I had to tell the chief of police we met online months ago." He looked out of the window like someone might suddenly appear and overhear his confession. "Sorry about that. I hope I didn't make you uncomfortable."

This was the problem with impulsiveness. Then you had to backpedal.

There was a pause, then she said, "You didn't. I was flattered. Men don't usually just spontaneously kiss me."

Then she was hanging around the wrong men. "I was serious about getting a drink. And if I can help you in any way with the show, let me know. I don't know Todd or I would talk to him."

"You can produce a whirlwind romance I can film and make the producer and Sadie happy."

Axl had an idea. Actually, maybe he could credit Chief Darcy with it. His boss had handed him an out. Now he could hand Leighton an out. It was a crazy idea. But it was what his grandfather would say was killing two birds with one stone. Saving both their asses in one fell swoop. "How about you film us?"

He was a practical guy. He wanted to spend time with Leighton, especially of the naked variety. He would get unlimited access to her for a week. Plus, neither of them would get fired or written up or busted on. He had no intention of getting married in real life, and he constantly had his mother on his ass about that. People were starting to question whether he was normal. If they thought he was with Leighton, and then the relationship tanked, they would leave him alone to lick his supposed wounds.

Pretending they were falling in love on camera was a diversionary tactic that could save both their jobs and let him live his life as a bachelor in peace. It would buy him a year at least from familial concern and harassment. Leighton would get the show she wanted to make her boss happy.

It was so simple and perfect it was kind of genius.

"Are you insane?" Leighton said, her voice cracking. "We can't do that!"

He pictured her full breasts, her narrow waist, her generous hips. He envisioned lifting that sundress over her head and having those curves all access. He wanted to flick his tongue between her legs, then drive his cock into her while gripping those soft thighs.

"Why not?"

LEIGHTON HAD an upset stomach from eating not one, but two, ice cream cones, and from anxiety churning her insides.

She had called around and hadn't found a replacement couple. Jill had told her not to post on social media because they would look desperate.

She felt pretty damn desperate.

In her hotel room, she was pacing back and forth in front of the window. Jackson had mentioned he had a lake view. She had a view of the dumpster, which seemed appropriate. Her career was a dumpster fire.

Now she was on the phone with Axl, who might have given her the best first kiss *ever*, except that it was under the worst circumstances possible. She would be in trouble at work with or without the kiss but it was not making the situation any better.

She couldn't tell if he was serious or not. The man sounded serious. He didn't seem like a prankster bullshit joke around kind of guy. But she didn't know him at all so she could be totally wrong. "Are you pulling my leg?" she asked him.

Axl actually gave a chuckle. "Sometimes you say things that sound like my grandpa. It's adorable."

It was actually a habit that annoyed her mother. She wanted her to be more on trend with her slang but it just wasn't her personality to be using the current catch phrase. "My father is seventy-five years old. I grew up on his phrasing. He's also German, so the combination is interesting, to say the least."

"Wow, your dad had you at forty-nine? I applaud his energy."

"He's a very good father," she said. "But not exactly the get-down-on-the-floor-and-play-dolls-with-his-daughter type." Back and forth she walked, agitated and distracted. "Though I don't really want to talk about my childhood when my future is at stake."

"Fair enough. So are you on board with my plan?"

"I don't understand your plan." She didn't.

"My plan is we have a whirlwind romance and we get married on Saturday."

Leighton needed to sit down. She also needed a stiff drink, the kind her father said would grow hair on your chest. She might also need some oxygen because she suddenly could not breathe.

"You want to get married?" she managed to choke out. Never, ever in her wildest dreams did she envision being pseudo proposed to over the phone by a man she barely knew.

"Well, fake married. We can use someone for the ceremony who isn't really ordained. Think about it. The ratings for a wedding after a quick romance will be huge."

It would be. There was no doubt about that. A clandestine love story. An immersion romance. Everyone would love it. Jill would love it. Viewers would eat it up.

Oddly, Leighton thought she might love it too. A whole week with Axl the police officer? Having him fawn over her and dote on her? What woman wouldn't want that?

But it was lying. She would be letting her friends and family and co-workers think that she had a hot boyfriend who was madly in love with her.

Though now that she thought about it, that was appealing too. Everyone always felt just a little sorry for her. Sorry that she wasn't skinny, sorry that she was shy, sorry that she didn't date a merry-go-round of men. It might not be the most humble quality to want everyone to see her as capable of making a man fall head over ass for her in a week flat, but there it was. She was never quite *enough* for everyone and this would make her seem like she was. It was tantalizing.

She had to question if she was a good enough actress, though, to convince people she wanted to get married on five days' notice. "I'm kind of a nervous Nellie if you haven't noticed," she said. "I'm not sure I can pull something like that off."

"I can take the lead."

"What's in this for you?" she asked because this was his home town. Having a romance and wedding that then ended as abruptly as it began would disrupt his life big time. "There could be big consequences to your personal life doing something like this."

"I care more about my job than my personal life. I don't really see myself getting married and having kids. I'm kind of the guy destined to go through life alone."

He didn't sound upset about that. Just matter of fact. But it made Leighton's heart melt in sympathy and understanding. She often felt that way about herself. That she was destined to be alone. Instantly, she felt calmer. Sinking onto the bed, she said, "Oh. I totally get that."

Everything inside her felt squishy when she thought about a man like Axl feeling lonely. The strong, stoic man who hid his emotions. The quintessential Minnesotan. Did his duty and went home to his empty house. Who didn't date because women wanted marriage eventually and he didn't want to mislead them.

"I can meet you at the hotel you're staying at tonight after my shift and we can talk about it."

Leighton shivered in anticipation. A fake romance meant very real kissing, and she had no qualms about that. "I thought you said you work until eleven."

"What better time to kindle a romance than at night?"

That made her feel warm. She wondered how real the fake would be. The kiss had been amazing. Axl had made her feel delicate and desirable and she had been caught up in the moment. "Sure. Okay. I can meet you in the hotel bar." It was poky and dark and a little dated but it would do. She wasn't ready to just invite Axl into her hotel room.

"Perfect. I'll be there by quarter after."

"Great, see you then." After Leighton ended the call she sat on her bed wondering what the heck she was supposed to do. Could she pull this off? A fake courtship. A hot cop. She touched her fingers to her lips, remembering the sizzle he had inspired in her with that kiss. "Holy moly, I'm in trouble."

This called for a best friend. She instructed her phone, "Call Zach."

Zach Collins had been her best friend since they were three and he had been a star on the pageant circuit, the only little boy who loved the glitz and glamour as much as the girls. His confidence had known no bounds and he did some fabulous routines to nineties classics like the Spice Girls and "What a Girl Wants" by Christina Aguilera. When Leighton had frozen on stage more than once, it had been Zach who had run out and held her hand and made up a routine on the spot for her to follow.

These days he was making a name for himself in makeup design on a hit TV show.

He was still fabulous.

He was still her source for confidence.

"Hey, sugar, what's up?" he said instead of a basic hello. "Are you rusticating in the wilds of Minnesota?"

"So, the groom bailed on next week's wedding and Jill is going to fire me if I don't find a replacement. Sadie thinks I need to 'bring it' more and I thought she was setting me up with some kind of test and I got pulled over and assumed the cop was a stripper and did a horrible job of flirting with him."

"I have no fucking clue what you just said to me. Start from the beginning. And Jill can suck my dick. She's not firing my Leighton."

His attitude always made her laugh. When it came to f bombs, he swore at a rate of a thousand to her one. "If Jill sucks your dick that will be the first woman to do that in how long?"

"Since tenth grade." He snorted. "It was a sacrificial suck. I felt sorry for her."

"How generous of you." She rolled her eyes.

"Explain to me what is going on. How can a cop be a stripper?"

Leighton started with the bachelorette party and explained how Axl had saved her from a panic attack.

"Hot *and* observant. I like. Go on."

"I didn't know it was a charity event. I thought he was a stripper, you know, nightly. So when he pulled me over I thought it was a joke."

"Cops that pull me over are never strippers. So disappointing."

In hindsight, it sounded kind of dumb. "I thought it was a setup. I acted like a freak, but what's even weirder is he kissed me. Now I'm getting fired if I don't produce a wedding and he is in trouble at work because my dashcam recorded everything. His solution is that we get married instead of Winnie and Todd."

"One, who the fuck are Winnie and Todd? Two, excuse me? Did you just say you're marrying the stripper cop?" His voice sounded scandalized, yet excited.

"He's not really a stripper. But yes, that's his solution. A fake wedding that everyone thinks is real after a whirlwind romance."

"That's so *now*. Totally on trend. I love it."

"You do?" Leighton bit her fingernail. "You don't think it's a horrible idea to fake a relationship for career advancement?"

"I want you to listen to yourself. You have betrayed your roots with that question. Faking a relationship for career advancement is mild compared to what some people in LA do."

"That's a valid point." Relationships might be scraping the surface of what people had faked.

"Is he cute or does he have a butterface?"

Leighton pictured those strong cheekbones, that stern jaw. His rich amber eyes. "Oh, he's good looking, trust me. In a real man sort of way, super masculine. Not a pretty boy. At all."

"That basically guarantees he won't be selfish in bed. Pretty boys are selfish. And oddly enough, ugly guys. You think they would try harder, but they don't. It's like they feel life owes them easy sex after being born with a hook nose. I've done the legwork on this so I know what I'm talking about."

"I'm not going to have sex with him." She wanted to, but she didn't think it was a good idea. She didn't trust herself to stay detached.

"I can't even with you right now. Why the actual fuck not?"

"Because it's a bad idea." She tried to sound firm.

"Wearing peach with your complexion is a bad idea. Having sex with a hot cop that you are having a fake relationship with sounds like your best idea ever."

"I can't wear peach?" Was he serious? She had a dozen items in her wardrobe that could classified as belonging to the peach family. She'd worn peach the night before.

Zach sighed. "No, you can't. But that's beside the point. Please have sex with the cop. For me."

That made her laugh. "Everything you just said is so wrong."

"I gotta go. A certain aging diva just showed up an hour late so now I have to rush. Love you."

"Love you, too."

"Fuck the cop!" he said and made kissing sounds. "Ciao."

Leighton pictured her ankles on Axl's shoulder.

Damn Jackson to hell for putting that imagery in her head.

She could not have sex with Axl. She didn't think. Probably not. Or she'd regret it. After enjoying it. Right?

No. No sex. But could she fake marry him?

This was going to give her the ultimate stage fright.

Sparkle, baby.

She took a deep breath.

Time to own the stage for the first time in her life.

FOUR

AXL DIDN'T bother to go home and change. He went straight to the hotel Leighton was staying at. It was a basic chain hotel in the mid-price range. There weren't a lot of options for accommodations in Beaver Bend but they weren't totally hick either. There was one high-end hotel and a couple of B&Bs in historic homes. Plus, lake cottages for rent that dotted the shoreline. He was surprised they weren't staying somewhere more upscale, but then again the show's star wasn't in town yet.

The bar was small and quiet, with one lone bartender, an older guy in his late sixties. He was chatting with Leighton, who was perched on a stool, her feet dangling freely. She was too short to reach the kick bar. She was also wearing denim shorts that showed a hell of a lot of leg. Her shirt was some kind of floral wrap thing. She was naturally very feminine and he found that very hot.

"Hi." When he approached her, he touched her back, rubbing a little with his thumb. It was presumptuous, he knew that. He did it anyway.

She turned and looked up at him with a smile. "Hi."

Her expression was soft. He had a feeling she thought he

was lonely given what he had said on the phone. It wasn't the slightest bit true. He loved being alone. In his house. On the lake. The quiet was something he craved after the military and the demands of his current job. He didn't need people and social interaction to constantly feed his energy. If anything, people drained him.

He'd seen too much to need mindless chatter to fill time.

But let her think what she wanted if he meant she was actually going to go along with this crazy idea of his. He had to admit it was insane. Yet, he had zero hesitation. Probably something he should dissect later, why he wanted a fake relationship but not a real one.

Not tonight.

Tonight was for coaxing and convincing Leighton.

He gave a nod to the bartender. "How's it going?"

"Quiet night here, and this lovely lady is talking to me, so I can't complain. Hope you had a quiet night too, Officer."

"We did."

"Can I get you a drink if you're off-duty?"

"I'll just take a Coke, thanks."

Leighton was drinking a glass of wine but it was nearly empty. "And another glass of wine for the lady, please."

She gave him a look. When the bartender moved down to reach for the chilled wine, she said, "Drink-pushing again. I'm not a girl who gets drunk and hooks up, just as a warning."

"I'm not getting you drunk to have sex with you." He gave her a slow smile. He was going to have sex with her at some point, but he did, in fact, want her totally sober. "That's not my style."

"What does that look mean?" she asked. "I can't read your expression."

"I'm thinking very dirty thoughts about you and how I don't want you drunk when I hear you say yes to me."

The bartender brought her wine and she sipped it. "You're very intense, do you know that, Axl?"

"I'm not intense. I'm just straightforward." He truly believed that. He spoke when he had something to say. When he said it, he meant it. Plain and simple.

"You also look at me like you're really interested in what I have to say."

"Of course I'm interested in what you have to say. Why ask a question if you aren't going to listen to the answer?"

"I find that refreshing." She gave a little laugh. "Attractive. I find it attractive."

"I find you attractive."

"So is this the first meeting of our mutual admiration club?"

"This is the start of getting to know each other." He imagined her growing up years were a hell of a lot different from his and he was curious about her life. About her.

"Then tell me about you, Axl Moore."

He didn't really want to go first, but at the same time, she'd asked so he would answer.

"I was born and raised here in Beaver Bend. Left to join the service. Spent four years in the marines, one deployment to Afghanistan. Came home, joined the force. My parents are still married and I have two sisters who are both married. One in Chicago, one here. I own my house because I like to do home improvement projects. I hang out with my friends from back when I was a kid. I fish, I like to go boating. I run for fun. That's it in a nutshell."

"You run for fun?" Leighton made a face. "Well, we differ on that. I only run if someone is chasing me, which explains my clearly not-so-skinny body." She smiled, and it wasn't an apologetic comment.

She didn't seem down on herself about her weight and he

was glad about that. She had the perfect shape, in his opinion. Womanly. "Your *hot* body."

Leighton blushed a little but she rolled her eyes. "I wasn't fishing for a compliment. But anyway, yes, I grew up in Beverly Hills. Yes, my parents are rich. Or rather, my father is rich, my mother rich by proxy. She met him when she was a cocktail waitress but they've been married for thirty years so whatever it was originally it definitely stuck. They both seem happy. I'm an introvert and it drives my mother crazy because she's always the life of the party. I like books, gardening, and interior design."

He could see she would enjoy quiet activities. Hell, like him. Different activities, but they were both drawn to quiet solitude. "No siblings? That's probably why you're an introvert. Though I have two sisters and I'm still an introvert, so I guess that means nothing."

"No siblings. One and done. Though my life would have been easier if my mother would have had a second daughter who wanted to do all the things my mother insisted I do. I despised just about all of them."

"Like what?"

"Singing lessons, dance lessons, acting lessons. Beauty pageants." Leighton shuddered. "The beauty pageants were horrible. Let's shove the chubby shy girl with a stutter on stage and that will help." She laughed. "I know my mother meant well, but I still carry the scars from those days." She held up her elbow for him to see. "Actual scars." She pointed to a white jagged line. "I fell off the stage trying to run away from the stares of all those parents and the judges, who were not impressed with me."

"That's terrible," Axl said, remembering clearly how panicked she'd looked on stage the night before. "I'm sorry. I can't imagine being forced to do something you don't like. Not to mention I don't really get the whole beauty pageants for toddlers thing."

"I think it's great for some kids. They really love it. Not me. My best friend Zach was a savant. He loved every minute of it and was amazing at performing. I was the deer in the headlights."

"I would rather rip my nails out with rusty plyers than be in a child beauty pageant."

Leighton gave him a grin. "And yet... you'll dance bare-chested for charity as an adult?"

Axl winced. "You've got me there." He put his hands up. "But I can't say that I enjoy it. That's too strong of a word. I can take it or leave it. My buddies Rick and Brandon like the atten-tion. Jesse is awkward as hell and I'm just kind of hanging out." He shrugged. "But I'll do anything for a friend."

There it was. That softening expression on her face again. "That's nice of you. You said your friend's wife died?"

He nodded. "Sullivan, who owns Tap That. Kendra died two years ago from breast cancer. She was only twenty-seven. Their son was two months old when she died. Finn's a cool kid. All of us guys try to spend some time with him when we can." When Sullivan wasn't being an asshole, which was more and more lately.

"Oh, my gosh, that's so heartbreaking. I think it's amazing that you're willing to do something to raise money in her memory."

"I feel a little bit like an idiot, I'm not going to lie. But there are worse things than having women yelling that I'm hot. I think the whole event goes to their head. It's like a positive mob mentality. Suddenly these four average guys in Beaver Bend, Minnesota are the hottest things they've ever seen. Except for Jesse, he's a pro hockey player, so that automatically elevates him. And actually, Brandon is loaded so maybe that makes him a notch above too. Rick has muscles on muscles on muscles. Shit, maybe I'm the only one who is average."

Not that he cared. He knew he wasn't classically good-looking. He was too rough around the edges and his mother always told him he looked too stern. That he needed to smile more. Lilly had told him he had Resting Bitch Face. Leighton thought he was intense, so Lilly and his mother were probably right. Whatever. It was his face. Like it or don't like it. There was nothing fake about him.

Except for this relationship he was planning to embark on with Leighton. He should feel uncomfortable with it being fake but he wasn't. He was doing this if she was willing.

Axl took a sip of his drink. When he turned, his knee bumped hers. It was an accident but he tensed when she gave a soft little gasp. That sound. God, she was so...ripe. Ready for a long night of him touching every inch of her.

"I can't speak for the women of this town but I come from a city of beautiful people and I hate to tell you this, but that is not true. Average is not what I would call you. You are, in fact, hot. Sorry." She gave a silly mocking shrug, lifting her shoulders almost to her ears. "You're going to have to learn to live with it, Officer Hottie."

"Very funny, Van Buren." But he wasn't actually annoyed. He thought she was downright adorable. He wanted to kiss her again.

"Van Buren? I don't think anyone has ever called me that." She looked taken aback.

"Really?" That amused him. "Who are you hanging around with? That's what any group of friends do, they call each other by their last names." It meant you belonged. Part of the inner circle. Maybe it was a guy thing. He'd spent a lot of his life in male-dominated environments. Hockey, the marines, the police department. Hell, even his fishing buddies were all guys.

"I wasn't aware we had a tight-knit friendship."

"I'd like to be friends." He shifted, placing his hand on the small of her back so he could lean closer to her. "I'd like to be more than friends. So, what do you think? Are we doing this thing or what?"

She stared at him, eyeing him with naked curiosity. "What thing are you referring to?"

He rubbed his thumb over her lower back. "You. Me. Telling the world we're a couple."

Axl couldn't think of anything more perfect than getting an entire week with her, no strings attached. Sure, it was mildly insane to let people think he was getting married. But once Leighton went home to LA and they staged a breakup everyone in his life would just be relieved because they would all think he was nuts for getting "married" on impulse. They would get off his back about not dating for years after something like this. The thought of buying time without nagging sounded fucking awesome.

He and Leighton would have fun. Have great sex. He'd save his ass at work and get his promotion to detective. She would keep her TV job.

What could go wrong?

"This is the most bananas thing I've ever done, but... yes," she said. "Let's do this." She fanned herself like the thought made her anxious.

His cock jumped, happy with her answer. "Then let's kiss to seal the deal."

She lowered her lashes and gave him a very sweet, very sexy smile. "I thought a handshake was how business deals are sealed."

"And they also say don't mix business with pleasure but I fully intend to ignore that." Axl brushed her blonde hair back off her face and cupped her cheek. "I've been thinking about your lips all day."

LEIGHTON HAD BEEN DOING the same. She hadn't been able to get that kiss up against her rental car out of her head all day. Having Axl gaze at her was like every fantasy she'd ever had springing to life. He was so damn intense. He looked at her like he was hungry for her. Like she was the only thing he saw right at that moment.

It made her feel appreciated. As if she was his only focus when he was talking to her. It was sexy as hell. He was sexy as hell. This didn't feel real. She didn't garner attention like this normally.

Her dating life had consisted of men who might be categorized as hipsters. She had always been drawn to glasses over biceps. Besides, muscle men were never into her. She was considered overweight by California standards and the one time a very fit guy had asked her out, he had spent the whole dinner date encouraging her to take up hiking, biking, running, and rock climbing. It had been annoying because she hated all those things and had no intention of ever pretending to like them.

Axl didn't look like he wanted to get her into the gym. He looked like he wanted to get her into bed.

"You're going to kiss me again, aren't you?" she asked, because she had basically implied she didn't want him to and now was regretting that more than anything ever in the history of her life.

"Absolutely. Unless you tell me you don't want me to. Say no and I will keep my lips to myself."

His hand on her back was very distracting. It was a light touch but my God, his hand was huge. It spanned almost the entire width of her lower back. The teasing strokes gave her goosebumps and her nipples had hardened. It was ridiculous that he could draw that kind of reaction from her with such light contact.

"I want you to," she said because everyone back home was always telling her they were living their best life and damn it, she wanted to live her best life.

She was one hundred percent certain her best life involved being kissed by Axl Moore.

He erased the distance between them and took her mouth in a sexy, deep kiss.

Actually, her best life probably included sex with this man.

Because the things his mouth did to her with a simple kiss were amazing and she couldn't even imagine how she could survive without knowing what it felt like to have him inside her.

Zach was right. She needed to get naked with Axl.

She practically *owed* it to herself.

Without any hesitation, she parted her lips for him and his tongue swept inside, teasing and tangling with hers. She closed her eyes and lost herself in the feel of their embrace. He had a manly scent. Like wood chips and skin. Just masculine and sexy as hell. She had read once that if you don't like your partner's scent you have a fifty percent higher chance of splitting up. Axl would have passed that test with flying colors. He smelled so much like a man should smell she wanted to lick him everywhere.

Her thoughts were so wild and scattered that she wrapped her arms around his neck to ground herself. To hold on to him. She was leaning forward, wanting more of him. All of him. His grip on her back tightened and his thigh pressed against hers. They were kissing deeper, more passionately, and she wanted him. All of him. She sighed, giving a little gasp when he unexpectedly nipped at her bottom lip.

"Leighton," he murmured.

She pulled back and opened her eyes. "Yes?" Oh, my God, whose voice was that? She sounded like a porn star. Breathy and excited.

Which she was. Breathy and excited, not a porn star.

"You drive me crazy."

Part of her was embarrassed. Part of her wondered if this was some kind of elaborate con. Men weren't driven to madness by her kisses. It just didn't happen. She had pleasant relationships with pleasant men. And not even recently. It had been eighteen months since she'd had a boyfriend. The last year she hadn't even dated much.

So this was all out of left field and really hard to wrap her head around.

But part of her, a part she hadn't even known existed, felt very pleased that she was having this effect on Axl. She felt naughty and sexy and she didn't want that sensation to go away.

"I don't think I've ever driven a man crazy before."

"Then you've been hanging around the wrong guys because you are so damn sexy. Your body was built to drive a man crazy."

That also pleased her. Because she knew for certain her body was not built for rock climbing.

Suddenly she realized the bartender was probably hearing every word they were saying. Awkward. Maybe that's what made her say, without warning, even to herself, "Do you want to go to my room? I feel like this moment should be private."

His eyes darkened with desire. His thumb brushed over her bottom lip. "Are you sure?"

She knew what he was actually asking. That if they went to her room and started kissing they might end up having sex and was she absolutely sure she wanted to do that? It wasn't her usual style. She wasn't impulsive and she wasn't a woman who could take what she wanted from a man and move on without a backward glance. In fact, she'd always envied those girls who could.

But she'd never met Axl Moore before.

She had damp panties from one kiss.

She wanted him.

There was no reason not to other than her pesky anxiety and right now, it was nonexistent. She should have damp palms, a tight throat, and heart palpitations the way she usually did when she was in an unexpected situation.

Right now, she felt nothing but a burgeoning desire that shocked her with its intensity.

"Yes," she said simply. "I'm sure."

He leaned forward and gave her a soft kiss. "You're beautiful."

Wow. Maybe her mother had hired him as a gigolo. Or Zach had. Because this was just crazy. Axl seemed so sincere, like he really thought she was gorgeous. She was cute. She wasn't gorgeous. Her mother was beautiful. Leighton benefitted from makeup contouring. It was that simple.

At the moment she didn't even care if he was a con artist, or a liar, or a male prostitute hired by a well-meaning loved one.

She just wanted to get that shirt off of him and feel those pecs.

She really didn't believe he was any of the above. Maybe that was naïve, but she didn't care. And hell, maybe Axl did think she was gorgeous. Everyone saw different things when they looked at someone. Maybe she spent too much time around body-conscious people.

There was something freeing about being with Axl. He made her want to throw caution to the wind.

Reaching behind her, she pulled her purse off of the chair where she had hung it, intending to pay for her wine. Axl was already dropping a twenty on the bartop. It didn't seem like enough for two glasses of wine, but she didn't want to sound rude.

Instead she made eye contact with the bartender, who was grinning, clearly entertained by the dynamic between her and Axl. He didn't seem to think he was getting stiffed on the tab. In fact, he gave Axl six singles back, which Axl used to return four to the bar. He was a decent tipper, she liked that.

Minnesota was much more affordable than LA, big shocker.

"Thank you," she said to the bartender. "And thank you," she added to Axl.

He gave her a wink.

She was pretty sure she'd just gotten pregnant.

That's how masculine he was.

He looked at her, winked, and bam. Everything inside her wanted to get naked and ride him.

Leighton never wanted to ride anything. Not horses, not the train, not a wave.

Yet she wanted to ride Axl.

She took one final sip of her wine and stood up.

She was going to the rodeo.

FIVE

AXL WASN'T sure what had changed Leighton's mind about having sex with him but he was not going to question it. He had asked her if she was sure, she'd said yes, and now it was go time. She actually looked determined. Like she had made up her mind and now she wanted to grab him with both hands.

He wasn't usually so aggressive with women. Out of his group of five friends, he was the least likely to have a one-night stand. He had in the past, but not nearly with the frequency of his buddies. It just wasn't his thing. He felt fucking awkward expecting a woman he just met to take her clothes off for him. But with Leighton it had been lust at first sight and he couldn't wait to get her naked.

Following her out of the bar, he thought about her attempts to be flirty with him when she thought he was a stripper sent to entrap her and he had to grin. "Hey, big boy" comments just weren't her style. He wasn't sure what her flirtation style was. Maybe straight forward, just like his.

Leighton was fast-walking, which was fine by him. He had a long stride and he wanted to get her alone as soon as possible.

She took him to the elevator. When the doors opened, he

put his hand on the small of her back again and followed her inside. She hit the button for the third floor and turned to say something to him. Whatever it was going to be got swallowed by his mouth dropping over hers. He kissed her hard, deep, dragging her up against his chest so he could feel the press of her luscious tits. He buried his other hand in her wavy hair, kissing her intently.

She gave a little moan and threw her arms up around his neck. She rose to her tiptoes. Axl lowered his arm behind her firm ass and hauled her up even tighter against him. They kissed like the end of the world was minutes away. Like everything depended on this kiss. With depth and passion and urgency. It was like with each press of their lips they were resuscitating each other.

He wasn't sure where that thought came from.

He just knew that he felt alive and in this moment.

Axl lifted her completely off the ground. She gasped.

"Oh, my God, put me down!"

But he ignored her. "Wrap your legs around me." He had her easily. He'd been working out since he was twelve. It wasn't a hardship to hold her up, his hands under her ass. He gave her a little bouncing lift to get her higher up on his hips. She was holding onto her shoulders and giving him a look of wide-eyed horror.

"Kiss me, Leighton," he murmured into her ear, before turning to meet her lips with his.

She kissed him obediently, her fingers trembling on the back of his neck. "This is insane," she whispered, pulling back slightly.

"Insanely hot."

"I can't argue with that."

He pursued her lips with his and they both got lost in the wild passionate embrace. Her curves were pressed everywhere against him, her tight ass resting on his forearms, her full tits crushed against his chest. He had a rock solid hard-on already.

The door swung open and he knew they should exit the elevator but that meant ending their kiss and he didn't want to do that.

"Oh, my God!" a strange voice said in shock.

Shit. They'd been caught. Axl dragged his mouth off of Leighton's and turned to see who was witness to their elevator intimacy.

It was two women in their sixties. Great. He was keeping it classy. "Sorry, we're just getting a room."

"I should hope so," the one with enormous black glasses and rich red lipstick said. "Maybe you should have ten minutes earlier."

She didn't actually look offended. She and her friend, who had short white spiked hair and a stylish scarf on, exchanged amused looks. "Are you a cop?" the second woman asked.

"Yes, ma'am. Off-duty, obviously." Why the hell hadn't he changed? This was not helping his current problem with his chief. There were most likely surveillance cameras in the elevator.

"I may need to get arrested," the first woman said and they both laughed.

Axl cleared his throat. He was mildly embarrassed, mostly amused. "Pardon us, ladies. Enjoy your evening." He reluctantly set Leighton back down onto the floor. She wobbled a little and he steadied her with his hands on her waist.

She tossed her hair back off of her face, her cheeks tinged pink.

The elevator door kept trying to close and Axl kept sticking his arm in front of it. Leighton darted past the women and he shifted, still holding the door until the pair of ladies moved inside the elevator.

"Have fun," one said.

"I can guarantee that, ma'am."

They both seemed to think that was hilarious. But he meant it very sincerely.

Leighton pressed her hands to her cheeks as the doors closed, leaving them alone in the hushed hallway. "I should be embarrassed."

"Don't be."

"I said I *should* be." She gave him a sly smile. "But I'm not totally embarrassed because I think they were jealous of me. What woman wouldn't be?"

Now he was the one who was actually mildly embarrassed. He cleared his throat. "Which way?"

"Left." She pointed and started walking. "Three twelve."

It was a short way which helped because his cock was rock hard and he wanted her naked yesterday.

Leighton fished her key card out of her purse and waved it in front of the touchpad. The green light went on and she opened the door and quickly stepped inside. Axl followed her, taking out his service revolver and setting it on the counter by the coffeemaker. Handcuffs went next to it.

Her eyes widened.

He realized he had probably just scared her. That looked sketchy as hell. Like he might do something threatening or abusive. He was about to tell her he would take them back down to his car when she sat down on the edge of her bed and started undoing her sandal strap.

"I've never been handcuffed before this afternoon," she said.

He wasn't going to lie. He was happy to hear that she wasn't getting cuffed on a regular basis, either criminally or sexually. But he wasn't sure whether she was freaked out right now or not. "I promise not to handcuff you tonight."

She actually gave a nervous laugh. "Oh, geez, that never entered my mind. I've led a very, uh, vanilla life."

Her sandal fell to the floor and she moved on to the second one, working at the buckle.

Axl felt a wave of tenderness toward her. Hell. He didn't know if she wanted this or not. Fuck. "I'll take the gun and the cuffs to the car. I don't want you to feel uncomfortable, Leighton."

But she shook her head. "That's okay. I think it's kind of hot, actually. I mean, just sitting there. Not, you know, in use."

All right then. Fuck yeah. Every time he thought he was going to have to rein it in she surprised him.

"I don't know what I'm doing," she said, her hand fluttering over her chest.

"Do whatever you want," he said. "There are no rules." Yanking his shirt out of his pants, he undid the buttons. She was perched on the edge of the bed now, just waiting for him to make a move. Fine by him. He moved in between her thighs, forcing her knees apart. She stared up at him, her chest rising and falling rapidly with her excited and anxious breathing.

Bending over, he cupped her cheeks and kissed her deeply. Instantly she wrapped her arms around her neck and kissed him back with enthusiasm. Axl eased her back down onto the bed, running his hand over the bare skin of her thigh. Her blonde hair fanned out on the mattress and her t-shirt was caught beneath her hip, stretching it so that her cleavage was on full display. It was a gorgeous sight. He couldn't resist caressing up her side and lightly brushing over that swell of pale skin peeking out at him before burying his hand in her hair.

He kissed her lips, her neck. Leighton tasted sweet like the wine she'd been drinking and he stroked his tongue over hers, wanting even more. Having her splayed out like this before him was an unexpected gift he hadn't even known he'd wanted until the second he'd seen her at Tap That. She was making little soft sounds of encouragement, her nails digging lightly into his arms.

Axl explored her every soft inch with his hands, teasing at her nipples through the fabric of her shirt, and dipping briefly between her thighs to stroke at the front of her denim shorts. Her waist fascinated him. She had such a full chest, curvy hips and tiny waist, that the S shape gave him endless entertainment. He could run his hands over that all night.

Her tank top gave under his sharp tug and he exposed her bra, a basic pink cotton that was straining against the volume of her tits. The bounce they gave at his movements made him groan just a little before he lowered his head to suck at the swell spilling out of her cup. It tasted as good as it looked. She gasped. Axl flipped both cups down simultaneously. Freed the nipples. Fuck yeah. The raspberry buds were taut and he drew one into his mouth, enjoying the sharp intake of breath from Leighton. He sucked and lathed it with his tongue, before moving to the other to give it the same treatment. Testing the weight of her tits, he cupped them, and felt his cock harden even further. Her chest was amazing.

He had to see her without the tank top and bra interfering. Sitting back, he shoved at the wrap thing she had on over her shirt. It was a sheer fabric and caught behind her. There was the unmistakable sound of a rip. "Fuck. Sorry, Leighton." Sometimes he didn't know his own strength. He had big hands.

She gave a soft laugh. "It's okay. Now I can say I've had a man rip my clothes off of me."

Damn. She'd let him off the hook and turned him on even further. "Is that a fantasy of yours?"

"It is now." She looked excited by the idea.

Holy. Shit. Axl didn't even hesitate. He ripped the wrap thing from both shoulders so that it was nothing to ease it off.

"Oh, my God," she murmured, sounding scandalized and aroused.

He took the neckline of her tank top and gave it the same treatment, turned on by the gesture. It was probably a first for him too, that he could remember. But damn, it was hot, just to tear that shirt apart and give himself full access to her luscious tits.

Shrugging out of his own shirt, he tossed it aside and went for the snap on her denim shorts. Those had to go. He tugged, she wiggled, which gave him a view of her tits he would remember to his dying day. He wanted to frame that perfection and hang it on his fucking living room wall.

Once her shorts were down, he shifted her thighs apart and lowered his head.

Every inch.

He was going to taste every inch of her.

LEIGHTON WAS in a haze of desire and shock. First he had taken her teasing about tearing her clothes literally and had torn her tank top like it nothing more than thin paper. His hands were huge, something she had noticed before, but not thought about what they were capable of. He had been using them so tenderly, stroking over her body. Then bam. Shirt gone.

It was very, very sexy.

She had never realized she would be so turned on by a manly man throwing his strength around. But first him picking her up in the elevator and now this? She wasn't sure her panties had ever been this damp. But it didn't matter because he whisked those off too and he had all her important parts freed of fabric.

It would be nice to feel his rock-solid chest, but before she could make a move to do that Axl was between her thighs placing a teasing kiss on her clit. She moaned, instinctively drawing her legs together a little. This wasn't something she did on the regular, have a man go down on her. It was the one time she felt a little self-conscious about her weight, which made her annoyed with herself. But the men she had dated had always been on the skinny side and seeing them buried in her full thighs brought to mind thoughts she didn't want to be having in the middle of sex. Her last boyfriend had been happy to be let off the hook. He had always offered it reluctantly, the way Zach did when she asked him for some of his fries. There was no way to say no without looking like a dick, so it was the world's most lukewarm yes.

Axl was different. When she started to draw her thighs together in an attempt to hide herself, he used those big ass and strong hands to ease them apart again. Then he kissed her like he meant it. First one side, then the other, sliding his tongue over the soft skin.

She shivered and relaxed a little. One glance down did not show her thighs swallowing him. It showed his dark hair, and his broad muscular shoulders spanning beyond her. When he glanced up at her, his nostrils were flared and expression intense.

"You taste so good," he said.

Oh, my. Leighton didn't even know what to say to that. Other than she loved Minnesota and its fresh air that grew giant men who made her feel like this. Wanton and delicious.

He dipped his head again and did things that she didn't even understand. He was everywhere down there, licking and stroking, his tongue driving her wild. The pads of his thumbs massaged her inner thighs, then her labia, teasing her apart so he could taste her more thoroughly. No man had ever shown so much dedication to her pleasure or enthusiasm for the one-sided gesture. But he seemed like he was enjoying almost as much as she was.

All Leighton could do was lie back and withstand the assault on her senses. He took her to the edge, and as if he sensed it, pulled back, pausing to blow gently on her.

"Don't stop," she begged because she was right there. "Please."

"I'm not going anywhere," he said. "But there's no rush either."

Easy for him to say. He wasn't being destroyed like she was. "I just need..."

He was leisurely teasing a finger at her opening and understandably, she was very wet. He was watching her, settled in between her thighs like he'd taken up permanent residence. "What do you need, baby?"

His tongue. His finger. His cock. An orgasm. In whatever order he preferred. Leighton didn't know how to express that to him so instead she just rocked her hips forward to encourage him to do something. Anything. It was torture. Delicious torture.

She wasn't used to asking for what she wanted. She couldn't force the words out now.

He slid a finger deep inside her and hooked it. Leighton shuddered in pleasure. Then he leaned forward and sucked gently on her clit. There it was. A sharp, intense orgasm sweeping her under as he continued to stroke inside her. "Axl," she breathed, gripping the bedding on either side of her hips. She needed something to hold onto as wave after wave of pleasure crashed over her.

When she finally relaxed her tense thighs and gave a sigh of satisfaction, he drew back and smiled up at her. It was a dirty, arrogant smile, and he rubbed his thumb and forefinger over his bottom lip. "Good?"

She nodded enthusiastically. "Good."

Axl rose to his feet and put his hand on the button of his pants. Leighton scissored her feet frantically to rid herself of her shorts entirely. They had still been trapped around her ankles. She couldn't believe this was happening to her. Axl looked like a stripper. He really did. His chest was broad and defined. His abs were rock solid and as he took his work pants down she saw a thick erection straining against black briefs.

That was promising.

She couldn't say she was picky. A man couldn't help what he was born with and she figured as long as someone knew how to use it, size didn't matter. But that didn't mean that she wasn't just a little curious and excited to feel Axl's hard and probably large cock inside her. Because yeah, she was. Swallowing hard, she was about to divest herself of her shredded kimono wrap when Axl removed his briefs and she saw all her convictions were about to be tested. Maybe size did matter because what she was looking at made all its predecessors pale in comparison.

Axl rolled on a condom he'd dug out of his wallet and turned back to her. He ran his hands over her, slowly, from her shoulders to her breasts, teasing at her nipples, making them harden. Leighton gave a soft moan, goosebumps raising on her flesh. He moved past her belly button, outlining her hips with both hands, before moving to cup her sex. "I love everything about your body," he said. "You're so gorgeous."

She felt his desire. It was reverberating off him, making her aroused even more if that were possible. It meant everything to her that he seemed happy with her just the way she was, instead of wanting something different or more. He didn't want her to perform. Just be herself. The feeling was definitely mutual. "And you're hot. I want to touch you."

She did. She wanted to run her hands over all those many muscles, including that thick erection.

"In a minute," he said.

Then without warning he grabbed her ankles and yanked her to the edge of the bed then raised them. "Put your feet on my shoulders," he urged. "I've been fantasizing about that ever since your co-worker mentioned it last night."

The sudden movement robbed her of breath, but it made a lightning bolt of heat shoot through her pussy. Not to mention the visual she now had in her head. At the time he'd said it, Jackson had mortified her but in the twenty-four hours since it had played in her head over and over to major distraction. "Me too. I'm looking forward to it."

She wasn't sure why she said that other than it was the truth but Axl gave a soft laugh. "So polite. But I'm glad to hear it."

"Jackson said by midnight but I think we missed that deadline."

Axl leaned over and glanced at his phone he had dropped on the nightstand. "11:52. Damn, I'm good."

She laughed, feeling giddy right along with turned on. "I'm impressed."

He lifted her feet so they rested on his shoulders. God, she needed to go back to yoga. She couldn't hold herself up but Axl seemed undeterred. He clapped an arm across her legs and held her solidly against him. The blood rushed to her head and she felt dizzy. Or maybe that was just the anticipation. With his other hand he used his fingers to test her dampness and to ease her apart.

Then he was there, teasing at her opening with the tip of his hard cock. He moved in torturous circles, slicking up his cock, easing it over her clit, then back to dip inside her again. Leighton moaned. "That feels good."

"I haven't even done anything yet."

"You've done a lot in my book." The oral sex, the orgasm...

whatever she might have said was lost on a gasp when he pushed into her with a hard, driving thrust.

To her complete and utter shock she had an orgasm. All that teasing with his tip, then feeling him fully stretch her, bumping her G spot, sent her over the cliff. She gave a cry of shock and pleasure and met his intense gaze.

"Holy shit," he said.

Her feelings exactly.

AXL HADN'T EXPECTED Leighton to come again so quickly and he had to say it was the hottest fucking thing he'd ever seen. Paired with the way her pussy was hot and tight around his cock he was just about drowning in pleasure. Her tits were bouncing with each hard thrust into her welcoming body and her plump lips were parted as she gave her cry faded into a low moan.

Her orgasm had her inner muscles clamping down on him, and a rush of warm moisture made for a slick, tight passage for him to bury himself in. He had been expecting something amazing with Leighton and fuck, this did not disappoint. Her hair was spread out around her head and above it from when he had dragged her down the length of the bed, her shirt torn open. Her bra dangled on her wrist and her nipples were pert and begging for his touch. He reached down with his free hand and teased one of the buds.

"Oh, shit, stop, Axl, I can't..." Her eyes were wide, her head turning back and forth like it was sensory overload.

He just held her legs tighter as she tried to escape and fucked her harder. She had the absolute perfect body for pounding into and he wanted her to take all his intensity.

"I can't," she said again. "I'm going to come..."

She said it like it was a bad thing. "So come, baby. Come again with my cock inside you."

Leighton's cheeks and her chest were stained pink and she looked dewy and sexy and stunned. Her eyes drifted closed when she let go. This time she exploded silently, head back, mouth open, tits arching up toward him.

It was amazing to watch. Everything he could have asked for. He held himself back, needing to make it last. He slowed down his tempo, wanting to enjoy her tight hot channel forever. This wasn't about anything other than right here, right now, with this woman. This fascinating, delicious woman who came apart so easily under his touch.

He drew out his pleasure, enjoying every stroke.

Then Leighton gave him a look. One that was so sexy, so beautiful, he lost his hold on his control. She looked *fierce*. Like he was fucking her so good she had gone next level.

Giving up the fight, he let go and exploded deep inside her pussy with a low growl. Man, she was so fucking good.

He gripped her hard as he plunged in and out, milking his pleasure, before he finally slowed down his rhythm. Axl relaxed his grip on her legs, easing them down onto the bed. She was breathing hard and he was more than a little stunned.

"That was crazy," he told her.

Caressing his hands over her legs, he eased out of her and sat down on the bed. "Damn."

"I second that." She tried to shift her torn shirt over her bare breasts but it was a futile effort. She only managed to cover one nipple.

Teasingly, he flipped the fabric back and forth. "Sorry about your shirt."

"I asked for it." Her eyelashes dropped demurely, as if she were shocked she said that.

"For which I am forever grateful." Axl eased her hair back off her cheek. "You have amazing tits, in case you didn't know that. An amazing body, all the way around. I may have mentioned that once or twice, but it bears repeating."

She looked mildly uncomfortable with the compliment, but she didn't protest, which he liked. "Thank you. You're not so bad yourself."

"Then every minute I've spent in the gym is worth it," he said, and he wasn't kidding.

"Oh, I mostly meant your cock," she said. "It's magnificent."

Axl almost choked on his tongue. He started laughing. "Thanks. Magnificent, huh? Wow."

"I mean, the rest of you is great too. What woman doesn't appreciate muscles? But yeah, you were given a gift with, you know."

Apparently saying cock twice was too much for her. "Dat dick? Is that what you mean?" He grinned at her.

"Something like that," she said. "But whatever you want to call, I really like it." Her cheeks turned pink.

Damn. Talk about an ego stroke. He couldn't ask for anything more.

Besides round two. "You want some water or a soft drink? I can go to the machine down the hall and get you something."

"I'll take a Diet, thanks."

With renewed energy he pushed himself up off the bed and dragged on his pants, not bothering with underwear. Sex always rejuvenated him and this had been sex on steroids. "I'll be back in a minute. Can I have your room key?"

"It's on the dresser."

Leighton looked like she didn't want to move anytime soon so he grabbed the key card and felt his pants pocket for his wallet and went down the hall. He found the soft drink machine and got himself three, plus one for Leighton. He was thirsty. He was hungry, but ordering a pizza at one in the morning to a woman's hotel room seemed like he might be pushing the boundaries of familiarity.

Of course, they were supposed to be getting married.

It was a crazy scheme for a couple of people who weren't particularly crazy.

But if tonight was any indication, he was going to get a hell of a fake honeymoon before they split up.

Balancing three of the bottles under his arm, he twisted the cap off the fourth and drank half of it walking down the hall back to Leighton's room. When he went back into the room she was emerging from the bathroom, a towel wrapped around her.

"Did you shower?" he asked, impressed. That was a light-ning quick shower for a woman, even if she clearly hadn't washed her hair.

"No. I just used the bathroom."

He set the bottles down next to his gun and handcuffs. "Then why are you wearing a towel?"

"Because my shirt is torn. I need to find a T-shirt in my suit-case." She clutched the towel tightly, like if she let go she'd expose herself to a roomful of children not the man she'd just had sex with. She looked nervous.

So basically, she didn't want to walk around naked. That was insane. If she really was his girlfriend he would beg her to wear as little clothing as possible at home. She really had a banging body. Considering where his mouth had been modesty seemed unnecessary but he wanted her to be comfortable so he didn't tease her about it.

Instead, he pulled her into his arms. "Before you get dressed, can I do something?"

"What's that?" she asked, looking up at him with a mixture of curiosity and desire.

Axl undid the knot she'd made of the towel between her breasts and tugged so it all came free. She was gloriously naked, warm still from sex. With his hands on her waist, he brought her up close against him so he could feel her full round tits pressed against his hard chest. "This. I wanted to do this." He brought his head down and kissed her. Not softly, but with possession.

His cock was hard and he wasn't done yet for the night. Axl let his hands drift lower so he could grip her sweet ass and bump her against him. She gave a soft moan and it was the most gratifying sound he'd ever heard.

"You like that?" he asked.

"Yes," she whispered.

While he kissed her deeply, sweeping his tongue over hers, he shifted one hand so that he could stroke over her soft folds. She leaned into his touch, which was immensely satisfying. He teased her apart and massaged over her clit and then eased a finger inside. Three strokes and he had her body damp for him.

Thank fucking hell his wallet was in arm's reach where he had just tossed it by the coffeemaker after getting the soft drinks. One handed he flipped it open and found a condom between the folds. Leighton was making delicate sounds of pleasure in the back of her throat, her head rested on his shoulder. He drove his finger deeper inside her.

"Oh, Axl," she said. She rocked a little onto his touch.

"Can I fuck you, Leighton? I want to fuck you against the wall."

She gasped, her head lifting up. Her eyes were glassy.

For a brief second he thought he had offended her, but she nodded enthusiastically.

"Yes. Yes, you can do that."

He didn't hesitate. He slapped a condom on, turned her body, and thrust his cock up deep inside her.

SIX

LEIGHTON LOST her ability to breathe. She had thought Axl was done for the night, because, well, she didn't know why she thought that. She had just assumed one and done. He'd hang out for a bit, then head home.

But now he had her back against the wall and was taking her with a sexy ferocity she had never experienced.

Dang, it felt so good to be right. The minute she had laid eyes on him she'd known he would be a man to take a woman against a wall. She just never dreamed she would be the one being taken. It was a very lucky break, because this was amazing. This was everything.

This was life.

She couldn't think, she couldn't react. All she could do was hold onto his shoulders, stand on her tiptoes, and be on the receiving end of the world's best dick. Award-winning, that's what it was.

He had one hand under her ass, holding her weight up, the other flat against the wall.

It must take amazing thigh muscles to do what he was and Leighton was impressed. And aroused. And oh so very grateful.

She didn't think she could have an orgasm in that position.

She was wrong.

It swept over her without warning, ripping through her like a gale force wind and she cried out. "Yes!"

"Yeah? Is that good? Do you want more?"

That was clearly a rhetorical question. "Yes, oh, yes."

She closed her eyes and tipped her head back against the wall so she could just feel the pleasure of each stroke, each rolling wave of her orgasm. She lost sense of time. It was just her and Axl and their bodies colliding until he paused, then exploded inside her.

"Leighton. Babe," he murmured, nuzzling her ear and nipping at the lobe.

She clung to his shoulders and took a deep breath to ground herself. She suddenly realized her calves were burning and she dropped her feet down to the floor. Which released the pressure in her muscles but also drove him deeper again inside her for a final shudder of pleasure for both of them.

When Axl pulled out and stepped back he backed into the coffee station, knocking his handcuffs onto the floor. He bent over and tossed them on the counter. "I'll save the cuffs for next time."

Next time? She shivered. Leighton tried to imagine being cuffed to Axl's bed. She would probably actually die of pleasure. She wasn't sure she could handle it. Though she was willing to try. "Whatever you say, Officer."

His head whipped around at her tone. She sounded seductive and she wasn't even trying. He just naturally drew that out of her. When she was with him, like this, she felt sexy.

"Damn, Leighton. Are you trying to kill me?"

"What good would that do me?" She shot him a grin while she retrieved her towel from the floor and wrapped it around herself. Naked was not her normal state of being. She reached for the soft drink bottle he had brought her and went to untwist the top.

But Axl took it from her and untwisted the top for her before handing it back.

It was oddly sweet. He didn't seem to think twice about it. She took a sip and watched him, wondering now what? She wasn't well versed in hotel hookups. In fact, this was her first. Did she ask him to stay or did that make it weird?

Anxiety started to chip away at her boneless bliss from sex.

Axl didn't wait for an invitation. He simply asked her. "Do you mind if I stay over? I don't feel like getting dressed and driving home. But if that makes you uncomfortable just tell me to go. Get the fuck out. Hit the bricks, Moore." The corner of his mouth turned up. "I have thick skin, so be honest."

"Of course you can stay." She wanted him to. Normally she loved to be alone because intimacy brought anxiety but tonight she wanted the sensation of a muscular man spooning her. It was an opportunity she would probably never get again and she was taking full frontal advantage. "I don't even steal the covers."

"I would let you. I sleep hot."

That she did not doubt.

Leighton went over to her suitcase and pulled out her satin nightgown.

"You have a nightgown?"

Axl sounded fascinated by that. She slipped it over her head and dropped it down until it hit the towel. Then she quickly whisked the towel away and shimmied the nightgown over her hips. She felt oddly shy around him. "What else would I sleep in?"

"A T-shirt. Or best of all, your skin." Axl laid down on the bed, very much naked and reached him hand out to her. "Please? Lose the nightgown for me. I want to feel you against me."

That made her nipples harden instantly. He was very hard to resist. She hesitated.

"Never mind. I'm sorry, that was pushy. The nightgown is pretty, keep it on."

Her heart softened. He had recognized her anxiousness again. He was very intuitive.

And because she didn't push, she wanted to give.

"No, it's fine." Off went the nightgown. Leighton quickly ripped the covers back and slid under them.

Axl followed suit and moved right up against her. He pulled her so that her butt pressed against his cock. He draped a hand over her midsection and cupped her breast.

Nothing about the position spoke of instant sleep. But she would willingly be bleary-eyed and cracked out tomorrow in exchange for a hot man hand on her nipple. Sometimes you had to eat the doughnut, so to speak.

Axl yawned in her ear. He kissed the back of her head.

And surprisingly, she fell asleep, deeply satisfied.

LEIGHTON HAD NEVER BEEN a morning person. It required six alarms, repeated dozing, and extreme willpower to haul herself out of bed each work day. If it wasn't for the technology of her phone and the programmed coffeemaker, she would have been fired a long time ago.

The knocking on the door was persistent and irritating and she wished whoever it was a painful and torturous death. But then somewhere between whimpers she remembered that she was in a hotel in Minnesota and this very possibly could be room service. She'd hung a card on her door the night before essentially begging for coffee at 7am. She'd circled what she wanted, but had also added some exclamation marks and a note politely requesting ten creamers. She liked cream. But now her eyes flew open as memories flooded back. Hot, delicious memories that had nothing to do with coffee.

She had put that card out before she had invited Axl Moore, the stripper cop, to her room. Yep. A quick glance over showed he was in her bed. His hand was lying heavy on her waist and she was naked. The knock came again. She was going to have to answer it and she was naked. Presumably he was naked too. She peeked under the sheet and saw not only was he naked, he was very much erect.

Her mouth watered and her nipples hardened.

She couldn't believe she got to play with *that* for the next few days.

It was like when she'd been given a science kit at age seven. Fascinating, explosive, and ultimately satisfying.

Dropping the sheet she met his gaze. Shit. Busted. He looked sleepy but also amused.

"See anything you like?" he asked, voice rumbling and low. His thumb started to stroke over her bare skin, right under her breast.

"Someone's at the door," she said, avoiding the question.

"Want me to answer it?" he asked. He started to pull himself up.

"No!" She put a hand on his chest. They were planning to fake a relationship, yes, but her sex life was none of the room service attendee's business. "I'll get it."

The pounding was more persistent.

Leighton slipped out of bed and looked for clothes, any clothes. Where the hell had she dropped her nightgown? Or that towel? Both were over by the bathroom and she didn't want to run across the room naked and bouncing with Axl watching. Instead, she snagged Axl's shirt off the floor and crammed her arms through it. It was big enough on her short stature that everything was covered to just above the knee. She managed one button closed on the way to the door, then settled for holding the fabric together as she pulled open the door, eager for a sip of coffee. Her throat was dry from all that moaning.

It wasn't an angel delivering caffeine in a cup.

It was Olivia, one of the *Wedding Crashers* crew. Olivia was around her age, was rail thin, and wore glasses with red frames that popped against her dark skin. She was adorably trendy and edgy with a super short hairstyle. But right now, that eyebrow with the piercing shot up. "Hey," she said. "You okay? We have a meeting scheduled that started ten minutes ago."

"Oh, shoot," Leighton said. "Is it eight already?" Did that mean her coffee had showed up and she'd slept right through that knock? It was possible. It had been a very late night. A very late and very satisfying night. Her cheeks flushed as she remembered Axl's tongue flicking over her clit.

"Yes," Olivia said. "And since you're never late I came to make sure you're not dead. I was picturing your ass murdered in the shower."

Yikes. "Nope. Not murdered." Leighton gave a laugh that sounded a little hysterical to her own ears. "Thanks, though. I appreciate the concern."

"Glad to see you're alive and well." Olivia eyed the patch on Axl's shirt that she was wearing.

It said Beaver Bend Police Dept.

Leighton cleared her throat and pulled the shirt tighter. "Be down in a few minutes. Tell everyone to start without me."

"Is that coffee?" Axl's sleepy and gravelly voice sounded perilously close behind her.

A glance back showed he had risen out of bed and was in nothing but his underwear, his short hair spiked up from sleeping and probably from the way she'd raked her hands through it during sex. Leighton turned back to Olivia, not sure what to say. "Not coffee," she called back to Axl. "Go back to bed. I'll order some."

"Damn," Olivia murmured, looking around Leighton to take in the muscular mostly naked man in her room. "Take your time, Leighton. I'll make up some bullshit to buy you some time."

"Thanks, I'll be down as soon as possible. Olivia, this is my, um, boyfriend, Axl." There was no time like the present to get this fake engagement rolling. "Sweetheart, this is Olivia, one of my co-workers. She's awesome and always has my back."

"Boyfriend?" Olivia exclaimed. "What the hell? You've been holding out on us, girl."

She shrugged. "It's a new thing. Sometimes you get swept away."

"Nice to meet you, Olivia," Axl said, coming up beside Leighton. He put one arm around her waist and reached out with his free hand to Olivia.

Olivia shook his head. "Yeah, you too. Leighton's a cool chick, you're a lucky guy."

Axl looked over at her and winked. "I know." Then he kissed the top of her head and wandered back into the hotel room.

It was absolutely surreal. Yet...awesome.

When did the shy girl ever get busted with a hottie in her room? The answer would be never. It was really kind of perfect. More amazing than it was embarrassing and she felt a certain pride that Axl was with her. She wouldn't have thought she would react that way, but apparently she was like any other woman when it came to scoring a hot guy.

"Okay, then," Olivia said. "See you whenever you can drag yourself away from that man of yours."

"Five minutes, I swear." Okay, maybe fifteen. She did need to get her hands on some coffee.

She closed the door behind Olivia and sighed. "I can't believe I slept this late, oh, my God. I need to jump in the shower."

Axl had found an in-room coffeemaker and was tearing open the packet of grounds. "Don't I even get a good morning?" He shot her a smile.

"Good morning." Leighton tried to rush past him to get to her suitcase.

Axl grabbed her, causing her to shriek involuntarily. "What are you doing?" She had to go to her meeting. She never missed meetings and she was skating on thin ice with her job.

"Getting my good morning kiss."

Leighton wanted a good morning kiss in theory. She wanted to feel like Axl really was her boyfriend, she could admit that. Even if she couldn't quite delude herself that thoroughly, she still wanted to enjoy a leisurely post-hookup morning together with the sexiest man she'd ever gotten naked with. But the reality was she needed to brush her teeth and her entire career was on the chopping block.

One kiss wouldn't hurt though. He looked determined.

Leighton shivered and dropped her white-knuckled grip on his uniform shirt she was wearing. "Make it quick, Officer."

He cupped her cheeks with his big, callused hands and studied her with those deep, amber eyes. "Whatever you say, California."

It wasn't a great nickname. But it was better than Amazon Prime.

Axl bent down and took her mouth in a kiss that made her wish they were marooned on a desert island with no clothes, a plethora of pineapples, and nothing but time.

The man could kiss.

And make her feel like she was the only woman in the world.

She pressed against him without thinking, her breasts warm on his hard chest.

Then he was pulling back and giving her a dirty, satisfied grin. He swatted her on the ass, startling her. "Go do your thing. I'll let myself out and I'll call you later so we can go to dinner and plan our week."

Leighton was actually disappointed. If he had coaxed her out of the shirt and up against the wall, she would not have objected. That was so not like her. Work came first. "Perfect," she lied.

She went to jump in the shower. Axl grabbed her arm again. She looked back at him in question.

"You better hurry before I change my mind and keep you in bed all day."

God, why was life filled with choices that sucked? Stay in bed, have multiple orgasms with a hot cop, lose your job. Be forced to move back in with your upset parents. Wind up taking some job you hate.

But, *orgasms*.

It gave her pause.

In the end, paying her rent won and she took the fastest shower possible. When she came out of the bathroom dressed and damp hair braided, face free of makeup, Axl was holding out a cup of coffee for her. Wow, now he really was perfect.

"Cream and sugar?" he asked.

"Cream, if they have it."

"Just the powder kind."

"I'll take it."

Axl doctored her coffee and handed it to her again. "Have a good day."

"Thanks, you too." This felt natural. So natural it veered into awkward. She did not know this man. None of this was real.

It was that thought that had her grabbing her purse and hightailing it out of there before she hovered too long expecting something.

"Look who decided to roll out of bed," Brad, the sound guy said, wearing a shit-eating grin as she walked into the boardroom.

She sheepishly sat down and sipped her coffee to avoid having to speak.

Jackson shook his head, like he was disappointed in her. "Told you that guy wanted in your pants."

"I thought he was your boyfriend," Olivia said.

"Boyfriend? They met in the bar last night. He's a stripper," Jackson said. "Didn't you see the video?"

Everything Jackson said annoyed her. "And what's wrong with wanting in my pants?" she asked. "If you wanted in someone's pants, all your friends would be all about that, telling her to go for it. But so for once in the time you've known me I decided to have some fun, and then you're going to judge me?" Geez, that ticked her off. Of course, she ruined her feminist declaration by saying, "Besides, Axl and I are dating."

"Dating?" Brad asked, eyebrows shooting up. "Is that what we're calling it these days?"

"Can everyone just leave the woman to her love life?" Olivia asked. "Hello, harassment."

"Whoa, whoa," Brad said, recoiling. "Let's not get crazy. I didn't say anything that could be misconstrued."

Leighton wished she were more like Olivia. Her co-worker just shut down comments. "Thanks, Olivia. Now, let's discuss how to salvage next Saturday."

"Can we hire a fake bride?" Olivia asked. "Because Jill is pissed."

"I have a better idea." Leighton took a deep breath and

threw it all on the table. "How about one of our own family here at *Wedding Crashers*?"

They all stared at her blankly.

"What do you mean?" Brad asked.

"Me. I think we should film my relationship with Axl and run a *Wedding Crashers* 'Love Behind the Scenes' type special." Her palms were sweating and she ran them down her dress under the table.

"But that's not a wedding. We're called *Wedding Crashers*." Olivia's look was skeptical. "Did you run this by Jill? What did she say?"

"I haven't spoken to her yet." Leighton jumped off the cliff. "But everyone loves a whirlwind romance that ends in a wedding."

"What do you mean?" Jackson asked, taking his glasses off and cleaning them on his shirttail.

Her stomach was churning and her throat was closing. "Axl and I are getting married. Hometown police officer meets LA girl, they fall in love. Viewers will eat it up." She was referring to this romance in third person because it was the only way she could say it without either bursting into hysterical panicked laughter or running out of the room like someone had set off a Roman candle on her ass.

No one spoke. The small boardroom was silent, save for the hum of the air conditioning. The table held Olivia's laptop and the remnants of Brad's breakfast pastry. Leighton was frozen in her rolling chair, hoping they were buying this.

"Are you crazy?" Olivia asked finally. "How long have you know this man? You can't be serious about marrying him. That is not like you. Not like you at all and I don't even know what to say now, because a hookup is your business and I have no opinion on that. But marrying a total stranger? Damn. I mean, just damn."

"I like it," Brad said. "Not that I have any say in anything. But I think Jill will be into it."

"I..." Jackson shrugged, looking bewildered. His mouth worked and he put his glasses back on. "I feel like anything I say right now will be wrong or misconstrued so I'm just going to say nothing."

"Excellent." Leighton breathed deeply through her nose, trying to quiet her anxiety. "I'll give Jill a ring."

"SO, I have something I need to tell you," Axl said, grabbing an apple out of the bowl on the kitchen table at his parents' house. He bit hard, steeling himself for his mother's reaction.

"You have cancer, don't you?" His mother, who had decided it was time to give up covering her gray hair, was midway through growing it out, giving it a certain Cruella de Vil quality. With the wrinkle of her nose and her harsh words, she was a little intimidating, even to him, a grown-ass man who had seen combat.

It didn't surprise Axl she'd leaped straight to life-threatening illness. That was just the way she was. "I do not have cancer or any other illness. Dad," he yelled. "Can you come in here?"

He didn't have a lot of time. He was supposed to be cooking dinner for Leighton, with a camera crew present. He was going to hate the camera, love spending time with her. He was still riding the high of sex with her and had no qualms about what he was about to say. It was time for Rob and Hillary to back off and let him live his life exactly the way he wanted to—which was as a single man indefinitely.

His father came wandering in, wearing a Vikings T-shirt. His father had recently retired after thirty-five years in construction and he was bored as shit by his own admission. His mother was still a school teacher but hadn't gone back for the new year yet.

"What's up, kid?" His dad clapped him on the back and wandered past him to open the refrigerator.

"Rob, it's four o'clock. Don't go snacking now. You won't want dinner."

His father sighed. He didn't argue. He just slammed the door to the fridge closed and looked miserable.

Axl knew his parents were happy in their marriage. He also knew that his father lived for the days when he could leave at four in the morning to go fishing and leave his wife's chatter behind. Axl was like his father in that regard and he did not want to be running away from a woman. He just wanted to live his life in peace. Which was why it was crucial for them to perceive his spontaneous "marriage" as a mistake.

"I met a girl and we're getting married Saturday. The girl in the video." That was his style. Cut to the chase. Straight forward. No sense in creating a build up.

His mother dropped the ceramic bowl she had been holding. It cracked in two solid pieces.

"Whoa." He bent down to pick it up. "Damn, that was a clean split."

"Axl Warren Moore." His mother's lip was trembling. "What on earth are you talking about?"

"I don't know any details about the wedding because she's planning it, but hopefully you can be there."

"Well. Congratulations, son." His father stuck his hand out. "Didn't know you were seeing anyone. Huh. Who's the lucky girl?"

"Her name is Leighton Van Buren. She's from LA." He shook his dad's outstretched hand. "Thanks, Dad. Appreciate it."

"What the hell are you talking about?" his mother shrieked,

repeating herself. "How do you know a woman from Los Angeles? You told me that girl is someone you're dating."

"We just met on Friday. She's in town to film a TV show as part of the production crew." He felt mildly guilty over his mother's distress but he figured give her a day or two and she'd be enthusiastically saying she'd always known he would marry someone from California or some shit like that. Hillary Moore was tough as nails but she could also spin anything to fit her narrative.

His father just nodded, like this was no particular issue. "When it's time it's time."

"Rob, are you nuts?" His mother glared at his father. "And Axl, you're clearly nuts. It's Sunday. How can you say you're marrying someone you met two days ago?" She made a sign of the cross.

Considering they were not Catholic and his mother had never been particularly religious, it was an intriguing and dramatic gesture. "Mom. I'm decisive. You know that."

"You cannot confuse lust with love."

Setting his apple down, he picked up her broken bowl and tossed it in the trash bin. "I'm twenty-nine years old. I know the difference, trust me."

"I don't know what to say."

"Say you'll be at the wedding. I can bring Leighton over this week to meet you." He had a feeling that wouldn't go over well with Leighton but if held her hand and did most of the talking he could bluster his way through it. Especially if the introductions took place somewhere public.

"We'll be there." His father opened the refrigerator again.

His mother slapped his father's arm. "Get out of the damn fridge!"

"Oh, by the way," Axl added, striving for casual. "The wedding is going to air on TV in a few months as part of

Leighton's show." He'd gotten a text from Leighton that her boss had given the plan the thumbs up.

"Now you've really lost it. You expect me to be on TV when I'm growing out my gray? I need another six months!"

That kind of amused him. "It's not a big deal. You look beautiful, Mom."

She gave him a look that would skin a live cat.

"So tell us about this girl," his father said. "What's so special about her that you're taking the plunge into marriage?"

Axl cleared his throat, bending over onto the kitchen island to give the question some thought. Yeah, this wasn't real. But Leighton was special. He thought about the way she looked lying on that big hotel bed, eyes rolling back in pleasure. He pictured her fear on that stage and how she had held on to him like he was her port in the rockiest storm. How she had tried to flirt with him to save his job. He smiled.

"She's intelligent, she's beautiful, she's sweet." He fingered his half-bitten apple and contemplated how she'd stumbled into his life and how crazy this all really was. No regrets though. He wanted every damn minute he could have with Leighton before she went home to her California lifestyle.

When he stood up, his mother's mouth was open and there were tears in her eyes.

"Your expression... Oh, my Lord, Axl. I've never seen you like this over a girl." She came over and hugged him. "Honey. Is this the one who can get you to open up? That's wonderful."

He took the hug begrudgingly. His mother's mission in life. To get him to "open up." Whatever that meant. He'd long ago given up on her just accepting that he was a guy who didn't want to talk about his feelings and that did not make him in need of therapy or baked goods. It made him a guy who worked shit out on his own. "All right. Let's not get gushy."

She smacked his arm and pulled back to wipe her eyes.

"When are we meeting this girl? And good Lord, what am I supposed to wear?"

So okay, he felt a tinge of guilt deceiving his mother.

But the bright side was he would be free to live out his life in peace as a bachelor who lived alone on the lake after this. No one would dream of bringing up dating if he'd been dumped by a new bride.

"Just don't wear black. It's not a funeral."

It might be his if his parents found out the truth.

But he'd seen combat and tackled criminals.

Fake-marrying an adorable blonde who tasted like sugar didn't scare him.

Much.

SEVEN

HAVING a cameraman and a lighting guy film him prepping steaks to throw on the grill didn't bother Axl as much as he thought it would. He was good at getting in the zone. He had great concentration skills, and an ability to block out distractions, which he employed right now as he seasoned the New York Strips on a plate on his butcher-block kitchen island. Leighton was next to him, tossing a salad, looking far less comfortable than he felt.

She was talking too fast. "So we'll do the interviews today and then tomorrow we have a cake tasting scheduled, is that okay? You should sync your calendar with mine so I don't schedule anything when you have to work."

He let her run down, like a windup toy. "Babe, I don't use the calendar on my phone so there's nothing to sync. I'll just text you my shifts. Cake tasting tomorrow is fine." He gave her a smile. "I like cake."

"You do? Or we could do doughnuts. Do you like doughnuts? Or cupcakes."

Her voice was starting to rise a little hysterically so Axl set down the container of sea salt down on the countertop. He reached over to Leighton and ran his thumb over her bottom lip. "I like you."

Leighton's lips parted in surprise and she said, "Oh." Color tinged her cheeks. "I like you too."

It was the truth. He did like her. She was pretty damn adorable. He leaned over the meat and gave her a soft kiss. "Let's go put these on the grill."

"Okay. Sure." She cleared her throat and turned to her co-workers. "We're stepping outside to put these on the grill. We'll be right back."

"Sure, no problem." Jackson lowered his camera.

"Do you want a beer or a soft drink or anything?" Axl asked the two guys.

"No, I'm good, thanks."

The other one, who had introduced himself as Brad, accepted a soft drink.

Axl held open his kitchen screen door and Leighton slipped through. He followed her, plate in hand, to the grill that was his pride and joy. It was both charcoal and gas, with a smoker. The granddaddy of grills. As he fired up the propane, he set the plate down and turned to Leighton. "You okay?" he asked quietly.

She nodded and sat down on his picnic table, crossing her legs. She was facing outward, not toward the table. "I'm fine. You?"

"Never better." With tongs he lifted the steaks onto the grill. "How do you like your meat?" He wasn't going to lie. He meant that to sound dirty.

Leighton eyed him. "You should know."

He laughed. "I have a good idea. As for your steak, how does medium rare sound?"

"That sounds perfect." She glanced around, settling back against the picnic table. "I like your place, Axl. It's so peaceful here."

"Thanks. That's what drew me to it too. I know the house isn't much, but it works for a single guy like me." His mother always threatened to decorate it for him, but she knew better than to come into his house and make it feminine. He'd burn it down before he'd let her turn his sanctuary into an ode to Tuscany. They were in Minnesota, not Italy, though his mother never seemed willing to admit that.

"I like the house. It's cozy."

"You mean small."

But she shook her head. "I mean cozy. You can really feel at home. I grew up in a twenty thousand square foot house. There is nothing homey about that, trust me."

"Damn. I can't even imagine that. My parents have a standard middle-America colonial. Enough room to get away from my sisters but not so much we could hide from each other." Axl flipped the steaks on the grill and added asparagus to the basket on the upper rack.

This felt like a normal date. Casual conversation. Getting to know someone. Getting to know Leighton. Except that he already knew her intimately. Had watched her eyes darken with pleasure. Had tasted her pussy and sank his cock inside her. It gave him an easiness around her he didn't normally feel on a first date. It was an odd juxtaposition.

"I always wanted sisters," Leighton said. "So desperately."

"You can have mine," he joked.

A funny look crossed her face that he couldn't interpret.

"I forgot my wine inside," she said, and quickly rose from the picnic table. "I'll be right back."

"I'll be in in two minutes," he told her. "I don't want to overcook these." Nothing worse in his opinion than taking all the pink out of a filet and making it tough to chew.

"Sure." Leighton ducked inside.

He wasn't sure she was comfortable with any of this but

they did engage in what he thought was easy conversation while they ate. Leighton smiled at him frequently and her voice had returned to a normal pitch. Maybe that was because cameras were off and Jackson and Brad ate with them. After they were finished eating, though, they sat on his couch facing the camera.

Leighton had given Jackson questions to ask them, which seemed ironic. Hopefully easy. She had given him instructions to rephrase the question in his answer, since Jackson asking the questions would be edited out.

The very first one didn't seem so hard. "What kind of wedding would be your dream wedding? Sky's the limit."

Axl shifted on the couch, his hand resting lightly on Leighton's thigh. "My dream wedding would be outdoors. Small, casual."

"That's it? Anything specific you want to add?" Leighton asked him.

"Nope."

She frowned at him. "That doesn't make for good TV, Axl. You need to have a specific request or demand. A deal breaker. Something over-the-top."

He could see her point. That was the way reality TV worked. If they were shopping for houses, they always had some crazy demand like a separate bedroom for their cat. The wedding shows must work the same way. "Okay. I would like to get married on my boat. The actual ceremony, I mean. And I want a wedding cake shaped like a fish. I think that would be cool."

Her face made it obvious she thought he was insane, but hey, she'd asked.

"I guess if there is a nautical theme the groom's cake could be a fish," she said reluctantly.

"Can it be red velvet? I love red velvet."

"It's going to look like the fish is bleeding."

But Axl shrugged. "I mean, the inside of a fish doesn't look like double fudge."

Her nose wrinkled, but she did look a little amused. He nudged her knee with his. "What's your idea of a dream wedding?"

"I've never thought about it."

"Liar." He could tell she had. It looked like an entire wedding start to finish was ready to burst forth from her tongue.

She turned to the camera, taking a deep breath, like she was steeling herself to be on camera. "My dream wedding would be in an English garden, with roses everywhere. An arch made of roses, rose petals in the aisle." She started to get in to it, her hand coming up to indicate the arch. "I want a bubble machine, pearl divers, and champagne bottles descending from the ceiling. Oh!" She turned to him excited. "The Queen Mary! Or the Titanic! That would be the perfect aquatic meets upscale theme."

"Baby, the Titanic sank and almost two thousand people died. I don't think a watery grave is a good wedding theme." Or a good theme for any party. Slightly too gruesome. Actually, a lot too fucking gruesome.

"True. Good point. But the Queen Mary would be amazing."

"Except that thing is docked in LA, correct?"

"It's my dream wedding," she said in protest. "We're just collecting ideas so the perfect surprise wedding for us can be planned."

"But you're planning it. So it's not a surprise."

She wrinkled her nose at him again. "You're not getting it."

"Nope. Not one bit." He reached out and tapped her nose. "But I trust you to get it. I'm just here for the cake and the wedding night."

Jackson laughed from behind the camera. "Dude. I feel ya on that."

"That's tacky," Leighton said.

"I never claimed to be classy." He gave her a grin. "Sure you want to marry me?"

Leighton bit her lip, as if she were giving it actual thought and this wasn't an elaborate scheme to save their asses at work. "Yes," she said softly. "I'm sure."

Without warning, he felt his gut twist. Her words sounded so sweet. So real. He studied those lips, so full and pink and perfect. Then he covered her mouth with his in a kiss that was spontaneous but also necessary. Because if he let her see into his eyes she might uncover the truth. That yes, he liked being alone. But he was also lonely.

He didn't admit that to himself very often. But he was resigned. Women he'd dated had made it damn clear he didn't give enough. If three girlfriends had all said that, the problem was clearly him.

Ignoring those thoughts, he pulled back and told her, "You can have anything you want. You deserve roses and champagne and fine dining."

His gut twisted again.

He must be hungry.

That was the only reasonable explanation.

Not that he was falling for Leighton for real.

LEIGHTON WAS HAVING trouble breathing and it had nothing to do with a panic attack. The way Axl looked at her was robbing her of all the air in her lungs. It reminded her of the way he had stared down at her intently when he was buried deep inside her body. She felt herself shift closer to him on the couch so that their legs were touching.

"This is your wedding too," she told him. "So fish cake it is." He was actually pretty sweet in addition to all his other very sexy attributes. God, she was so attracted to him. He made her feel beautiful and sensual and cherished. Her nipples were hardening in her bra and she felt the sudden urge to cross her legs to quiet the desire sparking to life.

Of course none of this was real, so it was easy for him to say she could have her roses.

That thought threw metaphorical ice water on her libido. She broke their eye contact and swiveled so she was facing the camera again. "Next question, Jackson."

"What is the most important part of the wedding day?"

It was a polarizing question. About fifty percent of the time it resulted in the groom saying something like "the open bar." It was designed to gauge if he was a sentimental groom or a joking kind of guy. That way they could direct events and footage to either go for the tears or to come off as a big entertaining party.

Axl surprised her. She had assumed he would make a joke about it. But he said, "The most important part of the wedding day is the first time you see the bride. That's a really special moment. Knowing this woman is willing to walk through life with you."

Leighton turned to him in amazement. Damn it. She was toast. The man was hot and romantic. It just wasn't fair. How was she supposed to stay distant and professional when he said things like that?

Maybe he was a phenomenal actor. But he seemed too straightforward of a man to be pulling platitudes out of his ass.

"How about you, Leighton?"

She'd forgotten Jackson and Brad existed. Now she removed her hand from Axl's knee, where it had mysteriously wound up and turned to the camera, forcing herself to not drop her eyes down. "The most important part of the wedding day is the vows.

My parents have been married for thirty years and I want the same thing. A lifetime."

It was the truth. She wanted all or nothing. No dabbling in marriage. No playing house with a boyfriend. Some people might want to live together indefinitely but that wasn't for her. She needed a commitment.

Ironic then, that Axl had already told her he had commitment issues. Or intended to stay single, anyway.

They were playing a dangerous game here.

She reminded herself what was at stake. Losing her job. Moving back in with her parents. Their disappointment. Her own feeling of failure. She'd never get another job in the industry because she had signed that damn non-compete clause. She could only work for another show if *Wedding Crashers* went off the air. Even if she was fired.

Fortunately, Jackson seemed to be in a hurry to get through the questions. Since he wasn't the one who usually asked them, he seemed annoyed by the role. His words were monotone.

"What colors do you want to showcase at your reception?"

"Blush," she said with zero hesitation.

"I don't even know what that is." Axl stretched out his legs and said, "I think blue is a good color. It's solid."

She wasn't sure what made a color "solid" but she was fine with it. "How about teal?"

"Is that blue?"

"Yes."

"Then sure."

"Blush and teal go well together."

"If you say so."

"I do." Leighton realized she had said the very thing that a bride was supposed to say at her wedding. She dragged her tongue across her bottom lip, moistening it.

Axl made a sound in the back of his throat.

"Where did you meet?" Jackson said.

"Online," Axl said.

"Bachelorette party," she said, at the exact same time.

"Neither one of those is a good answer," Brad called out, the beer Axl had offered him halfway to his lips.

Leighton was annoyed. When had he switched from soda to beer? And who said his opinion was needed here? "Next question."

"What's your favorite vacation?"

"Go first," she told Axl.

"Since I got back from my deployment in Afghanistan, I love the trees and water. Nothing with sand. So, my favorite vacation would be renting a cabin on the lake for a week. Fishing and boating."

"Leighton?"

"I've always wanted to see the gardens at Versailles."

She knew if this were a couple for one of their regular episodes she could take a few different angles. She could play up Axl's military background, making sure the Marines factored into the reception theme. As for her, she would use her beauty pageant background, even though she had sucked at it. Because viewers would like that whole debutante, rich girl angle. She would clearly emphasize the two worlds colliding in their background. A woodsy outdoors Minnesota ceremony followed by a classic LA nightclub reception.

But that was for two strangers and she didn't get the impression Axl wanted to be viewed as a military hero. She knew for damn sure she didn't want to be seen as a rich girl debutante. So she wasn't sure what she wanted to do for them. Fake or not, she wanted it to be an actual reflection of their tastes. Which was ridiculous. What difference did it make?

"Again, with the death theme," Axl said. "Weren't King Louis and Marie Antoinette killed there?"

Gardens had nothing to do with toppled kings. Not really. She made a sound of impatience. "Stop making me sound grue-some! I'm sure people have died on lakes too, you know. Drowning is a thing. Boating accidents are a thing."

"Fair enough." Axl turned to the camera. He was very natural facing it, which she thought was interesting. He was way more natural than she was. It hadn't even fazed him to be recorded while cooking. "So, here's the thing. Leighton is cham-pagne. I'm beer. In a can. But that's all wrapping. What's impor-tant is what's in here." He tapped his chest. "None of those things matter when there's love."

Damn it, he was so convincing. He was so believable that it made an ache build deep inside her, making her wish this was real on some level.

Her heart ached brutally. She wanted a true love. A future with a man who made her feel beautiful. More than she could have possibly realized.

Leighton jumped up with the urgency of when her mother had forced her on a colon cleanse at seventeen to lose weight.

"Interview over. Thanks, that was awesome, guys. Whew, I think we got some great footage."

Axl eyed her but he didn't protest. He just stood up and stretched leisurely, like he was stiff. Which made her think of when he was stiff the night before. That magnificent penis. Maybe even majestic. Oh, my. She didn't mean to look but involuntarily her eyes drifted down below his waistband. He wasn't hard but she could see the outline of his cock in those jeans. They were snug jeans. Just right jeans. Not pretty boy jeans but working man jeans. Not his gone fishing jeans but more like his date jeans.

Leighton shifted her eyes upward and saw Axl was watching her, amused. "If we're done, I'll drop you off at the hotel since I'm heading out for the night."

What? He was leaving? Leighton frowned. "Oh. Where are you going?"

Oh, Lord, that was so uncool. It was really none of her damn business.

But, well, she had just thought that since they'd both enjoyed sex the night before and everyone thought they were dating, he would want a repeat. She certainly did. They had limited time together. Six nights if her math was on point. That was approximately twelve orgasms that she would like to have, thank you very much.

"It's poker night with the guys. Every Sunday night. Unless it's football season. Then we watch the games together."

"I see." She didn't. Every Sunday? She loved Zach and he was her best friend but she didn't want a standing Sunday date with him. And he would tell her to get a life if she suggested anything of the kind to him. "Have fun then. I'm ready to go whenever the guys are."

As Jackson and Brad were packing up equipment Axl moved in close to her and bent over to murmur in her ear. "Tomorrow night I'm all yours if you want me."

She swallowed. "I want."

He laughed softly and straightened up. "Best thing I've heard all day."

In the car on the way to the hotel Axl said, "How do you think that interview went? I don't know how any of this stuff works so I couldn't really tell if I was giving the right answers or not."

How could he not know how adorable he was? His answers had been sweet and dangerous to her well-being. Because with every response, she had found herself thinking more and more how amazing it would be if any of this were real. It made her want to open her heart and tell him he was a special guy.

But all she said was, "I think the interview was good. You're actually really comfortable on camera."

"Must be my two-night stripping career. I'm good with an audience."

That made her laugh. But suddenly she wanted to know how many women he'd slept with in town. It wasn't a huge community. Was he a notorious bachelor who had screwed his way around Beaver Bend? She pictured him up on that stage, shirtless. Scratch that. She didn't want to know the answer to how popular he might be. "I promise we won't have to do a lot of interviews after this. The hard part is over."

"So now the fun stuff?" He gave a mocking fist pump. "Yes."

Leighton laughed. "How did I do? I was nervous."

"You did good, babe. But you should pull out some of your flirt moves to make it even more authentic."

She made a face. "You mean my awkward Officer Hottie moves? I'm pretty sure I suck at flirting."

"What? No, you don't. I want you to flirt with me." He squeezed her knee.

"I'll work on it." Though she didn't really want to "bring it" with Axl. She just wanted to be herself.

He smiled. "Just be yourself."

Damn. He was good.

Leighton was flustered. But she looked out the window to distract herself. It was a beautiful classic small town, with clapboard buildings and plenty of evidence of an outdoor adventure economy. There was a bait shop, a kayak shop, bike rental places, and several seafood restaurants. The boutiques all appeared to be catering to tourists as opposed to residents, with kitschy lamps and life preserver flotation devices repurposed as wall décor in the shop windows.

Axl had a truck and he was driving the speed limit. It was driving Leighton just a little crazy. Who drove the speed limit?

No one she knew. Huh. Maybe she had been speeding when he'd pulled her over. Determined not to fixate on how she might be falling for him, she gave him a tight smile. They were weaving slowly through the center of town. Like, really slowly.

Maybe he was driving so slow because he was a police officer who was already in trouble. He needed to toe the line. Maybe in a small town there was no rush to get anywhere.

Leighton enjoyed Axl's company but she really wanted to reach over and push his foot down harder on the gas pedal. Maybe she had a little more of the city girl in her than she realized. Years of frustrated driving on the freeway in LA, not moving. Going slow when you had the option to go fast was maddening.

"Hmm?" she said because he had said something she hadn't heard, too busy losing her mind.

"I said that you're beautiful."

That made her glance over at him, skeptical. "No, you didn't."

"You'll never know because you weren't listening to me."

Damn it. He was right. "I'm scouring venue locations."

"You're a terrible liar. Don't quit your day job for a career in poker."

"My mother always believes me."

"Then your mother is a much better liar than you."

Leighton laughed. "I don't believe you." She didn't. Her mother was disappointed in her in a lot of ways but she did believe that Leighton was honest. Which she was, for the most part. "This is a beautiful town. That is the truth."

"It is. It's cold as fuck in the winter but even that has its own sort of beauty. Do you like snow mobiles? Ice fishing?"

Leighton wanted to laugh again, riotously this time, but she held it in. "I haven't had a lot of experience with those, but I'm sure they're delightful." She would never find out though, because she was not going to be here in winter, nor would she be seeing him after the weekend.

Axl pulled into the hotel and parked his truck in the circular drive by the front doors. "Too bad I can't show you the charms of sitting inside a heated shed with a rod in a hole."

She wasn't sure if he meant that to sound dirty or not, but it sure in the hell did. "Did you hear what you just said? I'm not the only one who needs to work on my flirtation skills." She opened the door and shot him a smile over her shoulder.

The door slid open automatically but she was walking too fast. Her shoulder hit the glance and she bounced backwards. "Ow, shit."

Axl had already been out of his truck and walking around the front to say goodbye to her, but now he hustled over to her. "Are you okay?"

"Yes." She rubbed her shoulder. It didn't hurt as much as her ego. She could hear her mother scolding her as a toddler. *You're so clumsy, Leighton, Jesus.*

"These doors don't open very fast."

"Apparently not." She stepped back out onto the path in front of the doors so she didn't get slammed by it again. "Goodnight, Axl. Have fun at poker night."

"Thanks. You have a good night too." He looked like he wanted to say something, lingering there in front of her.

But then he just kissed her forehead. "Talk to you tomorrow."

Ew. She did not want a forehead kiss. She wanted a kiss full of passion and promise. An urgent kiss, like the ones he'd given her before. Was he already bored with her? She hoped not.

But it was in her nature to fret and she went up to her room and did just that. She went through the research list for Winnie's wedding to see if she could use any of the same vendors for her own event on Saturday. Nothing excited her or felt right. Axl wanted a boat or water and the restaurants she looked up online by the water didn't seem special enough.

Mostly though, she couldn't concentrate. She kept glancing over at the bed and wishing Axl were sprawled out on it, naked.

His house had surprised her. Much to her delight, it had been very clean and tidy. Sure, lacking in décor and a woman's touch, but it wasn't stark either. It was organized and masculine. It made her like him even more.

Which was a lot.

She called Zach. "I slept with him," she said by way of greeting.

"Good. Because I wasn't going to be able to be your friend anymore if you didn't bang a hot cop when you had a chance."

Leighton rolled her eyes. "You're a total liar."

"Was it worth it? Was it good?"

"Well." She took a deep breath. She had to tell Zach because if she didn't and he found out later he would most likely never forgive her. "It was amazing. As a matter of fact, it was the best sex I've ever had."

"Of course it was. It's the thrill of him being a cop, a fake stripper, the country air. You feeling sassy and dangerous by lying to everyone."

"Why do you make me sound so pathetic? Like I've never had an ounce of adventure in my life."

"How often do you have sex with men you just met and then pretend to marry him on TV? The sex could have sucked and you would convince yourself it didn't."

She had to call bullshit on that. "Oh, no, you can't convince me of that. This sex was fantastic. Multiple orgasms. Against the *wall*." She felt hot just remembering it. "I want to do it again and again and again."

Zach sounded gleeful. "Yum. So how long do you get to enjoy this paragon of the penis? When do you fake break up?"

"We just need to fake it until the episode films, which is in six days. Or five, depending on if you include Saturday or not." Her cheeks felt warm. That was a lot of sex. "Honestly, we haven't discussed a plan for afterward. I guess we need to." Yikes. She hadn't thought that far enough. Her brain had been stuck on sex and filming.

"Are you sure you can stand up there and pretend to marry someone?"

"It's going to be totally fine," she said. But the waver in her voice gave her away. Thinking about the wedding gave her a niggle of concern. She was sitting at the desk in her hotel room and she swiveled in the chair, swallowing hard. Admitting that out loud was out of the question. "I thought you of all people would be think this is a lark and I should just roll with it."

"I know you, that's why. You're falling for him," Zach said flatly. "You were right. I was wrong. You said you couldn't hookup without attaching and I pushed and now you've lost your mind. Now you're having some bridal fantasy that if you fake marry him, he'll for real marry you."

"I am not!" That had never once entered her mind. In fact, the very concept astonished her.

But now that he'd brought it up, the idea was just a little appealing. If she was going to get married someday, Axl would be a perfect fit. He was thoughtful and strong, and into the quieter pursuits in life, like her. He thought she was gorgeous.

No. *Stop it, Leighton.*

She could *not* go there.

Not a ball gown, but a mermaid style. That's what she wanted to wear when she stood across from Axl.

Damn it. She'd already gone there. Zach was right.

Old Glory roses. That's what she should carry. It was her love of roses and Axl's military background merged.

Of course she had fantasized about her own wedding she'd

have one day. She worked on a wedding show. She had just never pictured her groom as a hot guy with shoulders so broad he could pick her up and carry her around like it was no big deal.

It was lust crashing into like mixing with a hefty dose of longing for a fairy tale.

Leighton rubbed her forehead and told Zach, "You need to fly to Minnesota for my wedding. I may need an intervention."

EIGHT

IT WAS a risk telling the guys the truth, but they'd been through a lot with him. He could not look Sullivan, Jesse, and Rick in the eye if he lied to them about the true nature of his relationship with Leighton.

Brandon wasn't there, unfortunately. He only made it in from Chicago a few times a year.

They rotated houses for poker and tonight it was at Rick's. His apartment was over his auto body repair shop and like Axl's place, was pretty damn tidy for a guy in his late twenties. But Rick had good reason to be clean. He had custody of his little sister River, who was eleven, and he'd grown up with his dad being a hoarder, so he never wanted trash laying around. Jesse wasn't in town much during hockey season but in the summer he had a rental that he self-described as a flop house. He was not a tidy guy. Clothes fell off of Jesse and didn't move from their spot on the floor for months.

Sullivan was already pouring his second glass of whiskey as they sat around Rick's kitchen table. Axl eyed the bottle pointedly. Personally, he wasn't drinking at all because he had to work tomorrow. Rick had a beer, which he was nursing. Poker night wasn't about getting drunk, but Sullivan didn't seem to need much excuse to hit the bottle.

"We're only on our second hand, Sullivan. Ease up, brother."

"Fuck off," was his response. "I didn't ask for your opinion."

"Where's Finn tonight?" Axl asked. Sullivan's son was over two now and Axl worried about his buddy's ability to stay sober for his son. He knew Sullivan loved Finn with all his heart. But he also knew that Sullivan looked at Finn and missed Kendra painfully.

Sullivan didn't bother to answer him. He just threw some chips in his mouth and studied his cards with a scowl.

Rick said, "Sloane is sleeping over at Sullivan's. River is there too. Between my girlfriend and my sister that kid is going to be spoiled. They're always doting on him."

"Must be nice," Axl said, playing it casual, even though he was worried. But he was glad that Sloane and Rick spent a lot of time looking after Finn. "So I have news," he said, stretching his legs out under the table.

"Your balls finally dropped?" Sullivan asked, grinning at his own joke.

"Keep drinking and you'll keep being the only one who finds you funny." Axl put his cards face down on the table. "I'm getting married. Sort of."

No one said a damn word and Axl had to admit, he enjoyed the way his words hung in the air. He was never one to rock the boat. Ever.

"To who, a blow-up doll?" Rick asked. "You haven't even been hooking up with anyone, let alone dating."

"I know who." Sullivan looked at him over his whiskey glass, expression smug. "It's the California girl, isn't it?"

He nodded. "Yep."

"Who?" Jesse asked. "What California girl? Is that the chick in that video? You just met her."

"I may be booze soaked but I still know what's going on in my bar." Sullivan took a sip and set his glass down. "Lilly didn't think she was your type but I recognize a man on the hunt when I see one. But marriage? That definitely doesn't seem like your style, especially since, as Rick pointed out, you met her about a hot minute ago."

"I saw the video but I figured if you wanted to talk about it you would," Rick said. "I mean, other than us giving you shit in our group text. But marriage? Come on."

He didn't expect anything less. "Thanks, I appreciate that. Yes, this is Leighton from the video. And while I really dig her, no, this isn't a real marriage, so don't worry about me losing my mind. We're getting married on her show *Wedding Crashers*, to save both of our asses at work." Axl explained how he'd gotten reamed by the chief and how Leighton was on the verge of being fired. "The bonus beyond not getting fired is that now my parents will leave me the hell alone about getting married. It's constant. It ruins every damn holiday."

"Why does your mother want you to get married so bad?" Jesse asked, tossing a handful of nuts in his mouth. "My mother could care less if I do."

"Your mother thinks you're immature," Sullivan said.

Jesse glared at Sullivan. "No. I think she knows it's stupid for a guy who is on the road all the time to try to have a wife back home."

"I swear to God, my mother thinks I have PTSD and that a wife and kids will loosen me up." It was annoying beyond belief. "It drives me fucking crazy. I don't like throwing that term around. It's a real issue with a lot of servicemen and women. I just don't feel the need to talk unless I have something to say. Apparently that makes me 'not okay.' I have my flaws, man, but

I'm really pretty mentally stable, if I can say so myself. But my mom is worried that me being single means I am going to die alone, miserable."

"Your mom is intense, man. She always has been. That's why we could never hang out at your house as kids," Rick said.

That was true. They had always been at Sullivan's because his father let them do whatever the hell they wanted and his mother had skipped town ages before that, when Sullivan was a toddler. "My mother means well, but yeah. She's a lot to deal with."

"She's going to lose her shit when she finds out this is a con."

"She's never going to find out." He was confident in that. "I'm not admitting anything ever. Neither will Leighton. She has her own reasons to keep quiet."

"Marriage isn't a joke," Sullivan said.

"I know that," he said. He refused to be irritated by Sullivan's sullen attitude. His friend had good reason to defend the institution of marriage and he respected that, but this was his life, not Sullivan's. "But reality TV isn't real. That's the game and I feel like playing."

"How's the sex?" Rick asked with a grin. "Because that kiss on that video was clearly foreplay."

"None of your damn business." He wasn't the guy who told the juicy details about a woman he was dating. And if Leighton was anything, it was juicy.

"So, no chance you're going to fall for this girl?" Jesse asked.

Axl scoffed. "No."

He didn't think so. Not much.

And if he did, because okay, he was, he'd be fine. He wasn't the guy to fall head over ass.

It hadn't happened yet and he didn't see why it would.

That was the whole damn point.

He was emotionally shallow, to quote his last girlfriend.

There was no way he was going to end up wanting the marriage to be real.

And if he did, for whatever crazy reason, he wouldn't do that to Leighton.

He just wanted to enjoy today and worry about after the wedding after the damn wedding.

He put his hand down on the table. "Full house, assholes. I'm lucky this week."

And it had everything to do with meeting Leighton.

"OPEN YOUR MOUTH NICE AND WIDE," Axl urged her. "I have more for you."

Leighton shook her head at him, amused, and slightly embarrassed. He was holding a bite of cake on his fork in front of her lips. He knew precisely how his words sounded.

They were at Cakes by Autumn, sampling flavors for their wedding cake.

Autumn clearly got the innuendo as well. She was in her late twenties and she shot Axl a dirty look. "Stop embarrassing your fiancée," she told him. "You're the worst." She looked over at Leighton. "We went to school together. Axl and his friends were notorious for getting in trouble."

"That is not true," he said. "That was more Sullivan and Brandon. I kept my nose clean."

"I'm not sure I believe you," Leighton said, giving him a wry look. "What flavor is this before you shove it in my mouth?"

Her choice of words made Axl laugh and lift his eyebrows up and down. "It's true. I am, for the most part, a rule follower. And I have no idea what flavor this is."

She thought back to him actually following through and giving her a speeding ticket. Maybe she could believe he wasn't a troublemaker. She opened her mouth and Axl eased the fork between her lips gently.

"That's vanilla almond," Autumn said. "With a champagne buttercream frosting."

Flavor exploded in her mouth. Briefly, she closed her eyes before chewing and swallowing, savoring the sugary delight. "Mmm. That's really good, Autumn." She meant it and that was a substantial compliment coming from her. She had probably tasted two hundred cake flavors in her tenure as creative director.

Since the details of each couples' wedding were supposed to be a secret, part of their whirlwind wedding makeover, that included the cake. Which meant Leighton had to choose them for the majority of the episodes they filmed. Everyone on staff seemed to think that since she was already "overweight" she had nothing to lose by taking on the calories, so it fell on her to taste them. The size zero girls ran away from the cake like it was the physical manifestation of Satan.

Vanilla almond was a standard wedding flavor but Autumn's frosting was a cut above a lot of the samples Leighton had experienced. "What do you think?" she asked Axl.

"I want red velvet."

"You're getting the red velvet in your groom's cake. We need something else for the display cake."

"And what is the groom's cake going to be?" Autumn asked. She looked slightly panicked, probably because of the time-frame. "Am I doing that too?"

"Axl wants a fish. With red velvet," she told Autumn. "Can you do that?"

"That's going to look like fish guts," Autumn told Axl. "And your mother will freak out."

"Don't hate on my groom's cake." Axl switched plates,

pulling a chocolate sample in front of him. "And I'm a grown-ass man. I am not getting a cake to please my mother."

Autumn snorted. "I know your mother. That might be a mistake."

Uh-oh. Leighton's mouth felt dry. Damn sugar. She sipped the water Autumn had brought her. Axl hadn't said much about his parents. Not that they had spent a ton of time talking. She swallowed. Nope. Lump was still there. "Oh? How so?" she asked Autumn, striving for casual.

"Oh, Lord, you haven't met his mother yet, have you? You might want to do that ASAP." Autumn smiled. "Just a suggestion, I'm sure it will be fine."

Leighton turned to Axl but he looked unperturbed.

"What flavor is this?" he asked.

"Lemon with blueberry filling."

He made a face. "That's a no."

"Aren't you even going to try it?"

"Nope. I hate lemons."

"Then what do you want to try?" she asked him.

"Chocolate."

"Just plain chocolate?" Leighton was dubious about that.

"Everybody likes chocolate. Not everyone likes lemon."

She supposed she couldn't really argue with him on that point. Most people did love chocolate.

"Try this one," Autumn said, handing him another plate with a slice on it.

Axl put his fork through and came up with an enormous bite. He stuck it in his mouth and gave a thumbs up. "Now that's what I'm talking about."

"I need a tier that does not have cocoa in it," Leighton said. "Otherwise it's chocolate overload."

"I can do the top tier in anything you like."

"Almond would be great. As for the design, I want blush

rosettes, can you do that?" Leighton realized it might not be wise to tell Autumn what she actually wanted at her real wedding some day, but then again, she might never have a real wedding. Or if she did, her tastes might change by then. She might as well enjoy her fake reception.

"Sure, that would be gorgeous. Are you okay with that, Axl?"

"I don't know what any of that means but it's fine by me. It's the inside that counts."

Autumn put her hands to her chest. "Oh, my God, that's so romantic."

Leighton didn't think he meant it to be but she would let this love train roll. It was really kind of amazing how no one seemed to think they were certifiable for getting married two minutes after meeting.

That either meant that people were accepting of insta-love as a result of two decades of reality TV or they didn't believe it was real.

Which was possible. She didn't seem like Axl's type and he had grown up in Beaver Bend. He was a cop. Presumably a lot of people were familiar with his life. She really wasn't his type. She was buttoned up, he was buttoned down, despite his intensity. He liked casual, she was drawn to the formal.

Even if this were real, which it wasn't, it wouldn't work. It didn't matter that they were very similar, personality wise. He lived in Minnesota and she had a life in LA.

This was just good TV.

Leighton suddenly had a knot in her gut and it wasn't from an overload of sugar.

He reached over and wiped the corner of her mouth. "You have some chocolate there." Instead of licking his finger himself, he eased it between her lips. "How does that taste?"

Delicious. Like sex and a future she couldn't have.

Stunned at how upset that made her, she reared back so that his finger fell out of her mouth.

"Are you ready, Axl?" she asked, standing up so quickly her chair wobbled. "Autumn, I'll call you to confirm everything but it sounds like we've made a decision.

The tiny shop suddenly felt too warm and stifling. The scent of baked goods in the air was nauseating and the lemon-yellow walls were closing in on her.

"What's wrong?" Axl asked. "Are you okay?"

"I'm fine. I just got sick to my stomach all of sudden. It's hot in here." She waved her hand in front of her face and started toward the front door, abandoning her purse and her laptop. She'd come back for them in a minute. She needed fresh air desperately.

"Is she pregnant?" Autumn asked Axl in a low voice. "That's how I felt when I was first preggers with Jayden."

"No." But then he added. "I mean, I don't think so."

Of course she wasn't pregnant. They'd had sex once, two nights earlier. Well, sex twice two nights earlier. She was just on emotional overload. She'd warned Axl she wasn't that great of an actress. Keeping up this farce was intense and confusing. Between instead of acting, she actually wasn't. Being with Axl, she felt more like herself than she ever had with most men.

She was afraid she was going to lose track of what was real and what was fake.

Because it felt real.

As she burst out onto the sidewalk and took a deep breath of the summer air, she hated that the actual relationship was all fake.

Except her orgasms.

"Too much sugar," she told Axl when he followed her outside. "I'm not used to it, despite what my co-workers seem to think."

"Did you eat dinner?" he asked, looking concerned. "Let me go back in and get you some water."

"I ate some cheese and some grapes in a little pack from the hotel snack shop. Things have been crazy today trying to redo everything. I mean, I guess I could just give us Winnie's and Todd's wedding crash. I planned and booked everything six weeks ago. Filming couples with their requests is a formality for the cameras. Doing a wedding in three days isn't real." It was the logical thing to do, to just use the wedding she had already planned. Yet, she was resistant and she wasn't sure why. It shouldn't matter.

"If we just use someone else's wedding, aren't people going to figure that out? I mean, what did you have planned for them?" Axl put his hand on her back and rubbed gently.

His touch was very distracting. It was comforting and sweet. And maybe, just a little bit arousing. "A church wedding with the boy's choir performing and a barn reception."

Leighton pulled her phone out of her purse and started swiping. She had a folder filled with images of the color scheme and the venue. "What do you think?"

The church was a stone chapel. The barn was rustic. The elements she had employed were all natural. Wood arches, wine barrels, chandeliers twisted with ivy. The predominant color was a butter yellow, and an entire sunflower garden was supposed to be created at the entrance to the barn. It was a beautiful event, but it was not Leighton's personal style.

"It's okay. But I do not see you when I look at this."

Leighton glanced up at him, amused. "And how do you know what I would like?"

"You told me you like books and roses. Your clothes are always floral patterns in pastels. This isn't you," he said confidently.

He was right. But the fact that he had listened and paired

that with his own skills of observation was intriguing. Yet one more thing to like about him, damn it. "You're right. Rustic isn't me. But does it matter?"

"I think if we want to be believed it matters, yes."

"What do you want? Were you being honest in the interview yesterday?"

He shrugged. "I'm not picky. But yes, I was being honest."

"Then I guess I should change up some things. Any venue ideas? We can't get married in a church, obviously."

"I have the perfect place. Let's finish up with Autumn and I'll take you there."

Leighton tried to whip up some enthusiasm but honestly she was a little skeptical. Axl, the small town cop could not be an expert on unique and modern wedding venues. It was a science that she had down pat by now. Every episode she had to find something different, something breathtaking, something ground breaking. She'd done aquariums and riverboats and speakeasies. Barns, boats, and a basketball arena. It wasn't arrogant to assume she might have a leg up on Axl.

But after they ordered his plain chocolate cake with her lemon top tier, Axl drove her out of town along Lake Superior. He drove with a smug secretive smile on his face and his hand on her knee. Leighton prepared herself to get fake excited.

He turned down what looked like a private driveway. "We aren't trespassing, are we?"

"No, we're not trespassing. I know the guy who lives here. He's a vet from the Korean War and he's in his eighties. He's owned this property since the late fifties."

They were disappearing into a copse of trees, the concrete apron of the driveway giving way to gravel. A few hundred feet down the drive, the trees cleared and there was a small house. It was Victorian style. White with black shutters and lots of gingerbread trim. It was cute but Leighton wasn't sure where

Axl was going with this. It didn't seem like a wedding venue. Just some guy's house.

"What's your friend's name?"

"Bill Cove. We met at a Fourth of July parade and hit it off. He's a cool guy."

It was really sweet and cute that Axl was friends with a man three times his age.

She followed him out of the car and up the porch steps. There were two rockers on the porch and a number of flower pots, but there was nothing planted in them. She was worried she was going to have to tell Axl this wasn't going to work for the wedding and that somehow it would hurt Bill's feelings. Or heck, Axl's.

Axl knocked and Bill opened the door a minute later. "Hey, Axl, how's it going?" He put out his hand and they shook. He was tall and skinny with a warm smile. He was dressed in cargo shorts and a T-shirt, which for whatever reason, she wasn't expecting.

"Hey, Bill, good to see you. I hope you don't mind me dropping by without calling."

Bill rubbed his bald head, covered in liver spots. "What, because I'm so busy? Come on in, kid. Good to see you. Who's this lovely lady?"

Axl put his hand on the small of her back. "This is my, uh, fiancée, Leighton."

The words sounded awkward to her. He wasn't really selling it. But then again, she wasn't sure she could say that with a straight face either. "Getting married" seemed less intimate than "fiancée," which made her just silly and playing with semantics.

Bill's face registered surprise. "Fiancée? Wow, guess I've been out of the loop. I didn't know you were engaged. Nice to meet you, Leighton."

She took the hand he offered and shook. Bill had a strong grip and curious pale blue eyes. He was assessing her, that was clear. "Nice to meet you, too."

"Come on in, come in."

"Actually, I really wanted to show Leighton Soon-ja's garden. Leighton loves roses and we're looking for someplace special to get married."

Bill's expression changed. It softened. "I'd be honored to show you the garden. Come through the house and we'll go to the back."

"Thank you," Leighton said, now genuinely curious. A rose garden was the reason Axl had brought her here.

They stepped into the small house. It was decorated with midcentury modern furniture, which struck Leighton as fascinating. It was like Bill had moved in in the fifties, decorated it, and never changed it. Bill paused to pick up a photo and show it to her.

"My wife, Soon-ja, on our wedding day. She passed away nine months ago."

"Oh, she's beautiful, Bill. I'm so sorry for your loss." Soon-ja was stunning, her dark hair flipped up at the edges, her cheekbones striking. She was staring into the camera a bit mischievously. She had a small but full mouth and dark eyes.

"Thank you. I met her when I was twenty years old serving in Korea. I clapped eyes on her when she was my waitress in a restaurant and I knew she would be my wife."

"Really?" Leighton had always been skeptical of love at first sight. "Was that because she was pretty?"

Bill shook his head. "No, though obviously, I thought she was a looker. She turned heads everywhere we went. But that wasn't the only thing." He ran a shaky thumb over Soon-ja's face in the photo. "No. It was that when I saw her, I felt like I'd been punched in the gut. Our eyes met and I saw my entire future laid out in front of me. Wham. Life was never the same again."

That sounded so amazing. So...easy. Leighton had never felt that level of conviction in her entire life. "I take it she felt the same way?"

He gave a laugh. "Oh, hell no. I asked her out every day for a month before she agreed to go to dinner. And she said she only agreed to that so I would stop bugging her." Bill gave a grin. "But then I won her over with my incredible charm. Much like Axl here, I'm sure." He clapped Axl on the bicep.

Axl snorted. "I'm not sure what won Leighton over, to be honest. I'm not charming."

"It was your dance moves," she told him, amused. It was true. She'd seen him up on that stage and while it was not instant love, it was sure in the heck instant lust.

"Oh, shit," was Axl's opinion. "I'm lucky you even gave me the time of day then."

Leighton wasn't sure if he was serious or not. He had to know he looked good without his shirt on. But if anything, she hadn't believed he was serious about talking to her. "Axl bought me a drink and I refused to take it." It was weird talking about this when they weren't actually engaged. Or even dating. Yes, they'd had sex. But they weren't together. But she wanted Axl, and Bill, to know that Axl had proven himself a nice guy right from the beginning.

"Actually," she said. "The dancing caught my attention, but his kindness is what stuck with me." She eyed him, but he was looking at the photos on the wall. So she turned to Bill. "He saved me from a panic attack."

Axl cleared his throat. He looked embarrassed. "All right. Let's go see this garden."

"Take a compliment from your lady, geez."

"He's not that kind of guy," Leighton told Bill. "It's okay. He is romantic, though, whether he wants to admit it or not. He brought me here, didn't he?"

What Leighton could admit was that she liked Axl as a person. She liked that he wasn't bragging or patronizing or full of charming platitudes. He was the very definition of what you see is what you get. It was very appealing.

She wasn't sure what she was going to find in the back yard, but when she spotted the arched trellis dripping with pink roses, she felt her heart squeeze. Yep. Axl was a romantic. "Oh, Bill, it's beautiful," she said.

"You haven't seen anything yet," he told her, pride in his voice as he stepped off the back porch and started across the grass.

Leighton could see that in the distance, beyond the trellis, was the lake, dark and sprawling. The arch of the roses seemed to be framing a structure but it was hard to see because the density of foliage created a blanket of green and pink. The second they stepped under the arch she realized why. It wasn't a simple trellis. It was a series of trellises creating a hallway of roses. They were all around, a tapestry of perfumed blooms, encapsulating her in a cocoon of flowers. It was a veritable tunnel of roses. She gasped and turned in a full circle, and up above her, looking up in amazement at how the roses were carpeting the ceiling. Or rather, *creating* a ceiling.

"This is fantastic." Running her fingers gently over some of the open blooms, she felt Axl's eyes on her. Turning, she saw raw lust on his face. It made her gasp a second time because of the sheer raw desire in his expression.

"You look beautiful," he said.

"Thank you," she whispered. She could see he wanted to kiss her, and that if Bill weren't with them he would. Moistening her bottom lip, she looked away, unable to shield her feelings under that intense scrutiny. "Is this a greenhouse?"

There was a glass doorway at the end of the ten feet or so of roses.

"Yes, come on in." Bill opened the door. "This was Soon-ja's favorite spot. She would read in here for hours."

When Leighton followed him inside, she could see why Soon-ja would want to spend time there. It was like a fairytale. The entire greenhouse was constructed of old wooden windows. There were lights strung across the ceiling and several comfy couches and chairs with pink cushions. But the most extraordinary thing was the flowers.

They were growing everywhere. In pots, in boxes, on trellises. Among the flowers were whimsical water features burbling away. All the flowers were varying shades of pink, from the palest pink to a rich magenta. Leighton touched a bloom in awe. "Rose of Sharon."

Bill was standing with his hands on his hips and his jaw was working a little. Leighton realized how emotional it must be for him given that he had just lost his wife. "Good eye," he told her. "Rose of Sharon is the national flower of South Korea and I wanted something to remind Soon-ja of home. But turns out Rose of Sharon can't grow outside in Minnesota. Too damn cold here to survive the winter. So I started collecting old windows at garage sales and flea markets and garbage picking. In two years I had this greenhouse put together. Then we just started growing and it kept getting bigger and bigger. Now it's this."

"It's magical," she told him. "Seriously magical." Leighton reached behind her and snaked her fingers through Axl's. There was a lump in her throat and she wasn't sure what to say to him but she wanted to convey her appreciation for him bringing her there.

"Like I said, Leighton loves roses," Axl said, squeezing back. "That's why I wanted her to see this."

Bill didn't answer. He just went to the opposite end of

greenhouse from which they'd entered and opened a set of double doors. It framed a perfect view of Lake Superior.

"Wow," she said for the second time. She went to the open doors and found a little deck extending off the back of the greenhouse with yet more roses framing either side of the wooden platform. She could smell the water along with the heavy scent of all the flowers. The air on the deck was cool after the humidity of the greenhouse and she stood there for a minute, doing a full 360 degree turn. "This is perfect. We'll stand here," she said. "I'll walk up through the roses. Chairs here in the greenhouse. It will be tight but we can make it work. We will only have immediate family at the ceremony. The reception can be bigger." She could see it easily. It required barely any work, which was important on their timeframe.

She turned to Bill. "That's of course, if you don't mind us getting married here. I don't want to intrude on your special place."

In fact, she felt a little weird having a fake wedding in a place that celebrated a lifelong love. She didn't want Soon-ja haunting her from the afterlife. Which frankly, she would have every right to do.

"Of course you can get married here. I don't even come in here anymore. I have a gardener who takes care of the flowers now, but I can't bring myself to spend time here. It's a waste if no one is using it."

That made her feel a little better. If he sat there every day she wasn't sure she could bring herself to violate his space like that for the very mercenary reason of saving her job. "Thank you. We'll be careful and respectful with the space." She turned to Axl. "I mean, if you want to get married here."

The look he gave her made her nipples harden and a warm sensation pool between her thighs. He was undressing her with his eyes and it made her both completely aroused and flustered.

Seeing in her a garden should not be a turn on. That it was made her feel about as sexy as she ever had in her entire life.

"Yes," Axl said, and his voice was low, raw. "I will marry you here."

Suddenly Leighton wanted nothing more than for him to mean that. Because to be loved by a man like Axl would be like being swept away on a raging river. It would be endless passion and unfaltering loyalty.

It would be forever. Like Bill and Soon-ja.

And now she ached for something she hadn't even known she wanted.

Axl.

NINE

AXL WAS TORN between thinking that bringing Leighton to Soon-ja's garden was the biggest fucking mistake he'd ever made and the best decision ever.

She belonged here, among the thick walls of flowers, all pink, super feminine. Leighton was a girly-girl and he responded to that in the very depth of his masculine soul. He felt big and strong and protective around her. He liked her delicacy, her womanly curves, her sweet kindness.

The backdrop made him want to scoop Leighton up into his arms and haul her off to bed and never let her go.

Which was insane.

And the reason this was potentially a very dangerous mistake.

This was all fake and she was leaving in a week and he wasn't cut out for forever. And Leighton wanted that. He could see it in her eyes.

What he wanted was a short hot affair that let him feel everything and nothing. That sparked high then flamed out so he could go back to his ordinary bachelor life. The loner on the lake.

They were staring at each other, clearly both wishing they could strip each other down, when Bill cleared his throat. "So when is this shindig happening?"

Leighton broke their gaze and turned to Bill. Her cheeks were pink. "Saturday. If that's okay."

"This Saturday? Damn, kid, you don't let the grass grow under your feet."

"It's because it's going to be filmed for TV. Leighton works on a wedding show. Are you cool with the greenhouse being on TV?"

"TV? No kidding. That's fine. Soon-ja would be tickled by that, I'm sure. The last few years she was big into those Korean reality shows with all those young kids dating each other." Bill shook his head. "Not my thing. I like a good fishing show."

"Me too." Axl would rather rip his fingernails out than watch reality dating shows.

"I'll send a crew out here tomorrow," Leighton said, pulling her phone out. She started taking photos of the space. "Axl, do you have a tape measure?"

That made him laugh. "Now where would I have a tape measure? My pocket?" He patted his jeans. "Fresh out of tape measures."

"Don't be a smart aleck. I was more hopeful than anything."

"I can go get you one. I'm sure Bill has one lying around."

She made a face. "Don't worry about it. The crew can measure it tomorrow."

Leighton was on her phone, planning this wedding, looking very official. He thought she was cute. Adorable, actually. He grabbed her hand and pulled her to him.

He whispered in her ear, "You're very beautiful when you're organizing things."

She pulled away, tossing her hair back. "Hush."

Bill had sat down on a bench and Axl sat next to him,

watching Leighton take more pictures and touch foliage, and bend over to smell a flower.

If he ever were going to get married, it would be to a woman like Leighton. Or hell, Leighton.

The alien thought crept in with such randomness and authority Axl jumped back up off the bench.

He didn't know Leighton. This was a fake engagement. And he was never getting married. "Are you ready?" he asked her.

She shot him a startled look but nodded. "Yes."

She and Bill chatted, wrapping up their conversation and Leighton getting Bill's phone number so she could keep him abreast of the plans. Axl stepped out onto the back deck, needing air. He suddenly felt like he was being choked by flowers. Maybe like she had in the bakery. It was too much, crashing in on him. He'd spent the last few years convinced that he wasn't cut out for marriage and being totally cool with that and now without warning, he wasn't so sure anymore. He could see how fulfilling and enriching being married to a woman like Leighton could be, and it made him uneasy.

"Are you okay?" she asked him, putting her hand on his elbow.

He glanced down at her, not wanting her to read anything in his expression. He wasn't even sure how to process what he was feeling and he had no words to share that with her. "Yep. Totally fine. Let's go and give Bill his peace and quiet."

Without waiting for her, he took the outside path, not wanting to walk through Soon-ja's greenhouse again.

For the first time since he had come home from the service he regretted the solitary life he had forged for himself.

Because he was picturing a house on the lake with a garden for Leighton and a whole lot of time spent in bed together or out on his boat.

Which was insane because of all the women in Beaver

Bend, he had to go and picture a future with a chick from LA who was faking her relationship with him?

It was stupid.

Leighton was on her phone the whole drive back to his place. She was doing wedding shit. That wasn't the way she had put it, but it was how he thought of it. It sounded complicated. Lots of details, with flowers being flown in from California overnight and centerpieces from somewhere else. Lots of champagne. The whole thing sounded sadly lacking in beer but that was okay. He wasn't going to drink when he had a wedding night to look forward to, and when it might be his last time to see her gorgeous naked body.

She glanced up when he pulled in the driveway, so wrapped up she didn't even realize he hadn't been driving her to the hotel she was staying at. "Oh, you're not taking me back to the hotel?"

"I will later if you want." Axl felt a restless stirring inside him that only she could satisfy. "But my house was closer and I need to fuck you now."

Her jaw dropped. "I see."

He wanted her with an urgency that made his balls ache and his dick throb in his pants. His fists clenched on the steering wheel as he turned the truck off. Hell, he wanted to take her right here in the car. The ferocity of the need was overwhelming and unexpected. He wasn't a man who lost control of himself.

Other than his words, he didn't now either. He got out of the car, went around, and opened the passenger door for Leighton. She was eyeing him like he was a beast who might throw her on the hood of the truck. If she only knew how close he was to that.

"Are you angry?" she asked, slipping down out of the truck. "Did I do something wrong?"

That made him stop short. He reached out and cupped her

cheek. "Of course not. I don't want to hate fuck you. That's not my style."

"Then how do you want to, um, fuck me?" She pursed her lips.

He grinned. He couldn't help it. She had a way to shaking him loose. Lightening his mood. "How do you want it? Ladies' choice."

"Well. I hadn't been thinking about it in the last five minutes."

"So, think about it. It's sixty seconds to my bedroom." He dropped his hand and laced his fingers through hers. "Come here, babe."

She came willingly, though she did say, "I'm not sure I like being called 'babe.' Isn't every woman with every hookup called babe? We're supposed to be engaged."

"Do you have a nickname?" He didn't see what was wrong with babe but he could step it up if that's what she wanted.

Leighton made a face. "My boss calls me Amazon Prime because she says she can get anything from me in two days or less."

That made him laugh. Axl unlocked his front door. "That's as bad as what my co-workers call me. Ice Man. It's so stupid."

"Why are you Ice Man?" Leighton closed the door behind her as they entered his living room. "I don't get it."

"Allegedly I have no feelings. I'm cold."

Her head actually cocked slightly. "I don't know you very well, but what I'm seen in just a few days is the exact opposite of that. I wasn't making up a story when we were talking to Bill. I do think you're a nice guy. You are very compassionate."

So maybe there was something to his reputation because he felt uncomfortable as fuck talking about his so-called positive attributes. It was awkward. "I'll just keep the Ice Man label. It's all good." He tossed his cars on his coffee table and headed for the kitchen. "Do you want a drink? Water, a beer, anything?"

"Do you have some wine?" She wandered behind him, touching the art and pictures he had hanging on the wall.

It was a habit of hers. Her fingers just briefly brushed over things she was taking in, like she needed confirmation they were real. He wondered if she even knew she did it.

"I don't have any wine, sorry. I'm not really that big of a drinker. I have a six pack of beer, a bottle of vodka that has been in the freezer for two years, and a bottle tequila that I use maybe once a summer to make my mother a margarita."

"That's fine. I'll just take a water. What's your mother's name?"

"Hillary." He realized if they were put to any sort of test to see how well they knew each other they would fail miserably. "My father's name is Rob. How about you?"

"My mother's name is Barbara, though she doesn't go by that. She's Barbie." Leighton rolled her eyes, but she smiled at the same time. "Barbie suits her. She's very plastic. I don't mean that in a bad way, it's just the truth. My father's name is Dieter. I think I mentioned to you he's German."

"Do you speak German?" Axl opened the refrigerator and pulled out two bottles of water.

"Not at all."

"Damn. I wanted to hear you say something sexy in German."

"Sorry to disappoint you." She took a water from him and twisted the cap. She took a delicate little sip, then nearly destroyed him by taking the tip of her tongue and rimming the bottle.

His cock hardened. Enough of this chatting about their parents. Now was not the time. He wanted to get her naked. "Did you think of how you want me to fuck you?" he said, knowing she would blush, and knowing it would make him even harder.

She didn't disappoint. Her cheeks turned pink and she tucked her hair behind her ear. But then she turned the tables on him. "I want to fuck *you*. On top."

Holy shit. Axl groaned. "Then come on, babe. I mean Leighton." He would have to think about a better, unique nickname for her. "Miss California. You can have whatever you want."

She was wearing a dress again. Axl just reached out and lifted it over her head and tossed it on the kitchen counter.

"Axl!"

She was wearing a pale pink bra and panties. They were lace, which did not surprise him. Her bra was pressing her voluminous tits up into an even perkier position than they were naturally, which was pretty fucking perky, he had to say. She started to cross her arms over her chest, but he stopped her by taking both of her hands in his. "What?" he asked, as if he didn't know.

"You can't just rip my clothes off."

He grinned. "No?"

She realized what she had said and what she had asked him to do two nights before. "You know what I mean."

"Do you want me to strip for you? Would that make you more comfortable?" He lifted his hand to grab his shirt at the back of his neck.

"That's not stripping." She stepped back and leaned against the counter. "Stripping for real. Like you do at Tap That."

"That's for charity," he said, putting up a mild protest. Hell, he'd do whatever she wanted him to do.

But Leighton smiled. She put her elbows on his countertop, which did amazing things to her tits, which did amazing things to his libido.

"Do you need some music?" she asked.

"Doesn't matter. I can't really dance with it, so what difference does it make without it?" While he wasn't known for having an over-the-top sense of humor, he did feel comfortable enough with Leighton to pretend to pelvic thrust a few times. He rolled his hips.

She laughed. "Oh, my God."

He turned and bent over and shook his ass and looked at her over his shoulder. He was deadpan while doing it for added effect.

Now she was laughing really hard. "Please stop. That's just... no."

"No?" He straightened up. "Damn it. I was really enjoying that."

"You were not."

"Nope. Not at all. I don't need to show off."

Her eyes darkened. "No. You really don't. You have a presence without showing off."

He wasn't comfortable with her compliments. He didn't need his ego stroked. He undid the snap on his jeans. "I'm going to show you something."

She sank her teeth into her bottom lip, delicately. He wasn't sure Leighton knew how absolutely sexy she was. She wasn't body conscious or insecure, which he appreciated. But at the same time she didn't seem to understand the power she held. Axl unzipped and shoved his jeans down, kicking them off with zero finesse.

"I need tear-away pants," he joked.

"I don't think I could take that seriously at all." Leighton gave him a sweet smile. "I like you the way you are."

That shouldn't have any impact on him at all. And yet, it did. He felt something he couldn't quite pinpoint, which made him uncomfortable. "I like you too. Especially naked."

In his boxer briefs, Axl closed the space between them and reached out to run a finger along the swell of Leighton's breasts.

Then he bent over sucked that same swell of soft, warm flesh. She always smelled fantastic. Like flowers and sugar and something that was uniquely Leighton. Reaching around her back, he undid the clasp on her bra. Her tits burst forth, barely contained by the lace cups. He could spend all day touching her chest and never get tired of it. As he drew the straps of her bra down her arms, goosebumps rose of her skin. "Cold?" he murmured.

She shook her head. "The opposite."

"Hot? I would totally agree with that." He tossed her bra on the counter and cupped her breasts, teasing his thumbs over her nipples.

Leighton gave a soft gasp.

He kissed her, wanting that connection with her, wanting to see her eyes drift shut as he pressed his lips to hers. It was a moment he wanted to draw out, to savor, to use to stir up anticipation in both of them. She let go of the counter and wrapped her arms around his neck. She pressed her bare chest against his and rocked her hips ever-so-slightly so that her sex brushed against his cock.

Axl reached below her ass and hauled her right up off the floor.

LEIGHTON GASPED. "WHAT ARE YOU DOING?" she asked, digging her fingers into his shoulders and trying to find her balance. She was no yogi. She considered it a miracle she could actually ride a bike. Her core was for resting her iPad on, not for holding her entire body weight up.

"You said you wanted to be on top. The bed might be the

best place for that." He bit her ear lobe, drawing it between his lips.

She shivered. "You might have a point. I could walk though, you know."

"What would be the fun in that?" He took a couple of steps.

It was sexy to be carried. But it was also nerve-wracking. "If I was walking, you could see my ass," she told him. "I will walk sexy, I promise." If there were one thing beauty pageants and her mother had pressed upon her, it was that her walk was damn important. She could manage it with a certain amount of grace. Even sexiness.

Axl stopped and set her down. "Show me what you got, kid."

Relieved not to be carried, she ran her fingers across his chest, enjoying the way her pale pink fingernails looked against his hard muscles. Then she turned with a practiced pivot and started to walk, well aware that her panties formed a perfect little V on her ass. She was no size zero but she had a heart-shaped ass, thank you very much. It might not be suitable for a shift dress but it was designed for panties and sex from behind. Briefly, she rethought her requested position, but then decided against submitting a change request to Axl. She wanted to feel him sinking deep inside her while she held her palms flat onto his ripped abs.

Lost in her thoughts and ensuring that her booty moved enticingly for Axl's viewing pleasure, she realized she didn't know where his bedroom was. She paused to glance in the first room past the bathroom and discovered it was his workout room. But the brief hesitation had him impatient. Suddenly she jumped when he gave her ass a light smack.

"Keep moving, Van Buren."

Never in her life had anyone called her by her last name and it was as odd to her ear as the first time he'd done it. But it was strangely endearing. Axl had told her it was a privilege reserved for friends and in addition to the fact that he'd gone down on her like it was his job, she did think they were growing to be friends.

"Don't be so desperate," she told him as she started walking again and found his bedroom.

"Desperate? I refuse to be called desperate. Fuck that. I want you. I'm impatient. Not *desperate*."

Axl grabbed her playfully and Leighton screamed, laughing breathlessly as he tossed her onto the bed. She wasn't used to having a man be able to well, manhandle her. She felt very feminine and small beside him. "Stop being a beast."

"You want a beast?" Axl lifted his eyebrows up and down and climbed onto the bed over her. "I'll show you a beast."

He took his briefs down and Leighton covered her mouth in mock horror as his thick cock rose before her. "It's a huge, enormous, massive beast."

"Punk." He shook his head with a grin. "You're going to pay for that."

For some reason she thought of those handcuffs he carried. It had been terrifying when he'd clapped them on her by the side of the road. But what would that feel like here, in his bed? Her breathing increased rapidly and she felt her panties dampen.

"What dirty thoughts are you having, little Miss Leighton?"

"I'm picturing you punishing me."

Axl growled. "Damn. You're going to kill me." He bent over and took her nipple into his mouth.

Leighton stared down at the top of his dark hair and marveled at how fantastic it felt to have his tongue lathe over her tight nipple. He seemed to know instinctively when he had driven her to madness, and then he would shift to the other and start it all over again. She gripped his arms and let her head ease to the side while she was swept away by the concentrated pleasure.

But then when she realized she could just about orgasm from his skilled sucking and teasing, she realized she wanted to drive him as crazy as he did her. She wrapped her legs around him and said, "On your back now."

He paused to glance up at her. "Bossy. I like it."

She gave him a sassy smile. "If I could flip you right now I would. But I can't so I'm going to demand that you get on your back."

"Done." Axl grabbed her and rolled her with him when he went onto his back.

Leighton enjoyed the ride. He gripped her with firm hands and muscular thighs and when she tumbled over she landed on the hard plane of his chest.

"Now you have me right where you want me," he said, giving her ass a firm squeeze. "Torture me."

That was the plan. Leighton sat up, her thighs spread on either side of his. She took her time, exploring his body with her fingers and the palms of her hands. He had beard stubble that she brushed over, testing the coarseness of his hair, and flipping her thumb over his bottom lip. He tried to bite her finger but she drew it back quickly.

"Be still," she told him. "I want to play with you."

His eyebrows rose. "So I'm your toy? I like it."

"I don't get to feel muscles very often. I want to fully enjoy the experience."

"Don't forget the most important muscle."

She knew what he meant, of course, but she tried to wiggle her finger into his mouth. "Your tongue?"

He licked her finger. "No."

Leighton giggled. She couldn't believe that she could feel this way. Both turned on and amused. She felt... giddy with Axl.

Bending down she briefly sucked his nipple, then kissed her way down the pecs and to his rock-solid abs. His body was like a day at an amusement park. She just ran from one attraction to the next.

Below that sexy V on either side of his hips was the magnificent cock she had felt more than she had seen. Now she wanted to study him, from the tip on down the full shaft and to his tight balls. With each brush of her fingers down the silken skin he made a little sound in the back of his throat that pleased her. "Can I suck you?" she asked, already knowing the answer, but wanting to tease him the way he teased her.

"You can suck me for as long as you want. I'm not going anywhere."

The words squeezed her heart just a little. He didn't mean anything by them but her stupid, attach-too-easily heart wanted it to be otherwise.

"I've been thinking about this all day," she said, flicking the tip of her tongue over his tip.

Axl gave a little hiss but otherwise stayed still. "Really? You're a dirtier girl than I realized."

Instead of responding to that, she opened her mouth and slid down onto his shaft. It was a lot to handle but only in the best way possible. The growl he gave encouraged her to go as deep as she could. It made her feel powerful to have this strong man in her grip. She pulled back, letting her mouth pop off of him. When she took him again, she gripped him with her hand below her mouth and stroked with both.

"Leighton, that's good, babe. So good."

It was. She slid over him repeatedly, switching up the depth each time to keep him guessing. She shifted her hands down over his balls and cupped them, giving a small squeeze. So much of Axl was hard, rough, and holding his sensitive balls in her grip made her feel like she was completely in control. If that sharp inhale he gave was any indication, he seemed okay with that.

Axl gripped her head, tangling his hands in her hair. Her breasts felt heavy, her inner thighs aching. She was teasing him as much as she was herself, drawing out the anticipation.

She sucked him endlessly, lost in the rhythm, until he suddenly jerked her back off of his cock. "That's enough," he said, nostrils flaring.

"That was fun," she told him, wiping the moisture off her swollen lips.

"That was fucking hot." He shifted a little, trying to pull her up the bed. "Get on my cock, Leighton. I need to feel your pussy."

She was good at following directions.

Besides, she wanted him like she'd never wanted anything in her life.

Leighton shifted herself into position and then teased his cock over her slickness before easing onto him. She closed her eyes, overwhelmed by how amazing it felt to have him stretching her aching passage. "That is so...fantastic," she breathed.

"I agree one thousand percent." Axl gripped her hips and thrust up into her.

She sucked in a breath. She had wanted to move on him, though, so she flattened her palms on his chest. "Lie still."

He gave her a smirk. "Sorry." Axl put his hands behind his head. "I'll go hands free so I'm not tempted to touch you."

"I didn't say you can't touch me."

"I don't trust myself."

Leighton rolled her hips, enjoying the sensation of him fully embedded inside her. Her usual dates were well, less muscular, and being on top wasn't something she wanted to do often. Her last boyfriend had felt fragile beneath her and she had felt self-conscious, which of course destroyed any sort of sexy vibes.

But Axl was a whole different story.

There was nothing fragile about him. Not one single thing.

So she dug her nails into his chest and took what she wanted. She raised her hips and slid herself down onto him over and over, driving faster each time. Leaning slightly forward the way she was, she was teasing her clit against his flesh and between that and his thick cock stroking inside her, she exploded with a loud cry, head snapping back.

It was everything she had expected, craved, and more.

She closed her eyes and enjoyed the shivers of ecstasy spreading out from her core.

When she finally felt like she could breathe again, she opened her eyes. Axl was watching her with dark, intense eyes.

"Sit up," he commanded. "I want to see your body."

Even though she felt boneless, she mustered the energy to push herself up and off of him and settle back into a seated position on his cock. As he took over the rhythm, hands gripping her hips, Leighton raked her hair back off of her face, a strand stuck to her lip.

Axl moaned. She realized lifting her arms had given him an excellent view of her chest, which he clearly was fascinated by. She had to admit, she liked being ogled by him. It was deeply primal as was her response to it. It both turned her on and gave her even more confidence in her ability to drive him crazy. She bit her lip and lowered her hands to cup her breasts, squeezing them a little.

"That's not fair," he said, practically growling.

"What do you mean?"

"I want to last a long time and that is not helping."

Leighton rubbed her nipple.

"Fuck," was Axl's reaction, as he held her still with an iron grip, and exploded deep inside her.

Unexpectedly, it tripped off an orgasm in her. She didn't usually come twice in short order, so she cried out too, the pleasure sweeping away all thoughts.

Time and space seemed to stop and Leighton was stunned by how *complete* sex with Axl was.

Neither of them spoke. She slid off of him, spent, confused.

He lay still for a minute, breathing hard, before peeling off the condom. "Leighton?"

"Yes?" She was briefly scared by what he was going to say.

But then he said, "You would make a great porn star."

She burst out laughing. "Um, thank you? I guess? But remember what I told you about my pageant days. I'm not that great of a performer. What you see is all natural, not staged."

"Trust me, I meant it a compliment." He smacked her booty. "You have all the right moves and a body women pay money for."

That amused her. Axl really did seem to appreciate her the way she was and it was a unique experience to be with him. "I'll keep that in mind if I get fired."

"I don't mean actually *do* that." He gave a mock shudder. "I just mean you'd be really good at it because you're perfect. There's a huge difference."

"You're weird," was all she could think to say with a smile.

"I can't argue with that. I've spent a lot of my adult life with guys. I'm probably warped."

He certainly wasn't like the majority of men she had dated and she was enjoying how profoundly feminine he made her feel. "I think you're fine. I have no complaints."

"Good." Axl felt around and laced his fingers through hers. "What are you doing tomorrow? What to hang out until I have to go to work at three?"

Leighton only had about eighty-two million things to do but Axl looked so sexy and sleepy and *hard*, she couldn't resist him. "Sure. This will be our only day to spend time together. Wednesday I have to go find a wedding dress and meet with the caterer and the tent guy."

"The tent guy?" Axl shifted onto his side to look at her. "Are we going camping?"

She rolled her eyes at his joke. At least she thought it was a joke. It was possible he had no clue what she was referring to. "No. The greenhouse is for the ceremony. The reception will be down by the lake in an air-conditioned tent."

His eyebrows shot up. "They can do that? Damn."

"Oh, and I have to meet with the DJ. Then Thursday we have filming for the show and dinner with our parents. Then Friday, a dry run and rehearsal dinner."

"You never told me. How did your parents react?"

"Exactly as I imagined. My father was mildly interested and my mother was proud of me for 'following my heart.'" Leighton made air quotes. "I think they're just glad that I'm normal enough to be married. I think they were getting concerned that my introverted personality is too big of a turn-off for most men." She wasn't hurt by that. She knew they cared about her. They just didn't understand her and never would.

"Damn. That's harsh. And totally untrue."

"My mother just has a complete inability to see that anyone would be a different person than she is and be happy. But she does love me and she is very happy for me." Leighton felt no fear about the fallout when she had to pretend the marriage had failed. Her parents lived in a world impulse marriage and quickie divorces were not a big deal. They might be disappointed, and of course would be sad for her, but they wouldn't judge and she appreciated that about them.

Her mother only judged her eyebrows, not anything outrageous she might do.

"It sounds like our mothers both like to be the center of attention. They might wind up in a smackdown."

Alarm bells clanged in her head. She had never even thought about that. "Oh, Lord, you don't really think they'll hate each other, do you?"

"I don't think they'll hate each other. But I think they will try to out-talk each other, given what you've told me about your mom. I'm guessing our fathers will get along just fine."

Leighton felt the press of panic.

Then she remembered it did not matter in the slightest if the parents did not get along. It was one and done. One dinner and then never again.

She should feel relieved by that but mostly she felt flustered and hot.

Apparently Axl agreed. He was eyeing her like he wanted to take her. *Mine. Now.*

"What kind of dress are you going to wear? Promise me there will be lots of cleavage." He hooked a finger on the street covering her chest and tugged it down. "It would be a shame not to display these gorgeous tits to full advantage."

Leighton tried not to be turned on by the arousal in his voice and failed miserably. "It's a wedding, not a night out at the strip club. Cleavage will be tasteful."

"Well, that sucks." Axl punched his pillow in protest.

She laughed. "But you get to play with the cleavage after the wedding. Just keep that in mind."

"What are you wearing *under* the dress?"

She had no idea. "It's a secret." Even from her. She needed advice but she was scared to ask Zach. She didn't trust his taste level. Barbie would happily give her recommendations but that was not a conversation Leighton wanted to have with her mother. That meant she was going to have a phone a friend. A lifeline. She had three close girlfriends and she had to invite them to the wedding anyway.

Which reminded her. She had so much to do. This was insane.

Normally she didn't get freaked out by To-Do Lists but this was different and she refused to think about why that was the case.

"Oh, my God," she wailed. "I have so much to do it's bananas."

Axl laughed with a snort, which he covered with a cough. "You're bananas, because you use words like 'bananas' in that context. Relax. This is your job and you're damn good at it, remember? I know you can do this."

She loved that about him. Her mother, Sadie, they were always telling her she needed to be *more*. Axl thought she was fine just the way she was. There was nothing to bring because she already had it. She took a deep breath and concentrated on not panicking.

He reached out and stroked her cheek. "Hey. You've got this."

What she was starting to really wish was that she had him. He felt like her champion. The guy who always knew the right thing to say to her.

"Thanks," she murmured. Then before she said something he wouldn't want to hear and she shouldn't say, she rolled over to face away from him and resolutely closed her eyes.

"Are we done cuddling?" he asked, even as he shifted in to spoon her.

"I have to get some sleep or I'll hate myself tomorrow."

Almost as much as she hated herself for falling for Axl.

TEN

"IT'S REALLY BEAUTIFUL HERE," Leighton said as Axl jumped on board his boat and held out a hand to help her.

"The most beautiful thing I see is you," he said, and it wasn't a line. He meant it. Not only was she beautiful, she was special. He didn't take women out on his boat because the lake was his sanctuary. His quiet space. He loved the lake but he had some serious like going on for Leighton.

She rolled her eyes but she gave him an indulgent smile as he took his hand. "You need to get out of Minnesota more often."

"I've been out of Minnesota. Don't plan on doing it again."

Leighton was gingerly stepping onto the boat in shorts and an off-the-shoulder sweater. She had pristine white shoes on that he suspected would no longer be white when he dropped her at the hotel later.

"You're never leaving Minnesota?"

"For vacations, sure. But I don't plan on living anywhere else."

Leighton gave a squeak and jumped delicately onto the boat

deck from the marina dock. She dropped his hand and put hers on her hips. "Nice rig. Is that what you call it?"

"No. I call it a boat."

She rolled her eyes again. It was her favorite expression, it seemed. "My parents have a sailboat. I'm seaworthy."

That made him smile. She had the cutest way of talking. There was something almost retro about Leighton that made him think his grandmother would have really liked her. His father's mother, who had passed away the year before. She had been very feminine, into all things domestic. She had run her house with an organizational skill that rivaled his drill sergeant.

"Good to know you won't get seasick."

Leighton rubbed her arms. "It's a little chilly. The temperature took a nose dive."

"I think it's sixty-eight degrees, so yeah, that's a little cold for August. Do you want a sweatshirt? I have one below."

"Maybe I should."

Axl went and retrieved his sweatshirt for her. Leighton peeled off her sweater, something he wasn't expecting her to do. She had on a tank top underneath but it clung tight to her curves. He went for her. But she was on to him and she darted out of the way.

"No touching!" she said, laughing. "We're in broad daylight and there are a half dozen people here at this marina. Behave yourself, Officer Hottie."

"That's boring." He went for her again but she dragged his sweatshirt over her head and everything good in the world disappeared beneath blue cotton. Damn it.

She ignored that comment. "Sadie thinks we should do a video post."

The real world intruded and he did not like that. "For what?"

"For the show." She anxiously chewed her fingernail.

"Sure." He liked the idea of having something concrete. A captured moment of him and Leighton. One, for him to see whenever he wanted. Two, to show the world that even if it was fake, there was something real there too. A connection. A friendship, sexual chemistry.

"Ugh, you're supposed to say no."

He laughed. "What? Why?"

"I hate doing videos or taking photos. Everyone has these amazing Instagram shots and I'm over here stuttering and squinting."

"Leighton."

"What?"

"You're bananas." He used one of her catch phrases. "Give me your phone and we'll do a video and everyone will think we're fucking adorable and you know why?"

She shook her head. "Why?"

"Because we are adorable."

Leighton pulled her phone out of her shorts pocket and smoothed her hair back. She handed it to him without a word.

"Come here beside me with the water in the background," he said.

She obediently stood next to her. He had them on her phone screen.

"So here we are out on Lake Superior on this sunny Minnesota day. It's three days until our wedding, so we're super excited. Aren't we?"

Leighton nodded. "Yes."

Axl glanced over at her, amused. "Don't sound so excited."

"I've very excited." She sounded stilted and nervous.

He looked back at her phone. "She's cold. Minnesota is rough on a California girl."

He could see on the screen she still looked uncomfortable.

So he kissed the side of her face. "I'm happy to have Leighton out on the lake with me." That was true.

"Ack!" she said, wrinkling her nose and pulling away.

That made him laugh. "No sugar for me?"

She turned and stared up at him. What he saw there, in her eyes, made his laughter cut off. "Of course there's sugar for you."

He forgot about the camera. All he saw was her and something that damn near made his heart skip a beat. She opened her mouth to speak.

The wind whipped her hair across her face and broke the moment.

Leighton swiped at it.

"See you Saturday," Axl said to the phone. "We're going below deck." He ended the video.

Leighton shook her head. "Oh, my God, doing that is so hard. How do people film themselves constantly?"

"I have no idea. Not my scene. Normally. Until I met you." He grinned and moved to undo the rope tying the boat to the dock. "Now I kiss you streaming."

"That makes two of us. I told you about my beauty pageant failures. I like being a behind-the-scenes kind of girl." Leighton sat down on a cushion.

"When I'm not at work, I'm a leave-me-alone kind of guy." Axl went to the wheel. "Okay, I'm starting this thing up." He didn't want to talk. He just wanted to enjoy the sun and the lake and a beautiful woman.

He didn't want to stop and think about why he not only did he not mind Leighton on his boat, he liked having her there. She was a cute little skipper to his captain.

Which meant he was fucking nuts.

She was going back to LA and her Beverly Hills life and he was staying right here, on the lake. It didn't matter that nothing about Leighton screamed California other than her blonde hair and her very put-together outfits. She wasn't arrogant or spoiled or attention-seeking or any of those other stereotypes he had in his head about rich girls from LA. But that was still her home and where she'd grown up and where she belonged, presumably.

Axl drove along the coast until he got to town and then he cut the engine so they could float past Beaver Bend.

"This is a good perspective on the town," she said, lifting her sunglasses up and scanning the shore. "It's a cute place. Like what I imagine Norway looking like."

"Sure, if Norway was drowning in coffee shops and pet groomers."

Leighton laughed. "And what's wrong with coffee and clean dogs?"

"Nothing." Axl sat back, tipping his head to feel the sun on his face. "Someday I'd like a dog. But I'm concerned I work too much. Dogs need time and attention."

"I've never had a dog. My dad is allergic. I would love a dog. But my apartment is too small and I travel too much."

"I always had a dog growing up." That was how he envisioned his life as an old man. Fishing with his dog. It was a good goal.

Leighton cocked her head. She was sitting with her ankles crossed. "Why do I picture you as being the kid who ran wild in the woods slapping down branches with a stick?"

"That's probably pretty accurate. In the summer, I was in the woods. The winter, the ice rink. I loved playing hockey." Leighton didn't strike him as a kid who had played sports. "What did you do as a kid?"

"I read books. And suffered through dance lessons and singing lessons. I went on a few acting auditions at my mother's insistence but I cried at one and ran out on another so my mother gave up on that dream."

He felt bad for young Leighton. She must have been terrified. "Why do parents want to live vicariously through their kids? I don't get that."

"Do you want kids, Axl?" she asked, and her voice sounded wistful.

It told him right away that she wanted a family.

"It's not what I ever pictured for myself, no," he said truthfully and reluctantly. He hated when women pressed him, wanting an explanation. He didn't even know entirely why. He'd just never seen that future for himself and he never wanted to defend that to anyone. "But I don't know," he said. "Never say never. I like kids, just never thought I would be good at raising them."

Leighton didn't ask him intrusive questions.

She just said, "I completely disagree. I think you'd be a great dad."

"Thanks." Axl didn't know what else to say. He didn't want to talk about feelings. And he didn't want her to compliment him. It wasn't his thing. But he reluctantly asked, needing to hear her answer. "Do you want kids?"

"I'm not sure, honestly. I do, in theory. But in reality, it seems scary. Too much responsibility. I would be happy with a dog."

That wasn't the response he had thought he would get. He thought she would say she wanted kids as soon as possible and that he would be able to dismiss him and her as never working because they weren't on the same page.

But damn, it seemed like they were exactly on the same page.

It wasn't something he should even be thinking about at all but he was. He couldn't shake it. Leighton was special and it felt like the ground underneath him was rocking like this boat.

"How did you get your name?" he asked, wanting to change to the subject.

"It's my mother's maiden name."

"That makes sense."

"How about you?"

This story always kind of amused him, even though he'd hated his name growing up. Well, he should say it amused him now, because the idea of his mother throwing caution to the wind seemed so out of character. As a kid, he'd hated when they would tell this story because it was just embarrassing. "Back in the day, my mother was a huge Guns N' Roses fan. Apparently, I was conceived in a hotel room after the concert. My parents had to drive to Wisconsin for the show and my mother was *really* excited. My father likes to joke he had an appetite for seduction, which is awkward as shit when you're sixteen and he tells that at holiday dinners."

Leighton looked confused. "I don't get it."

"It was the Appetite for Destruction tour. So, my dad's lame joke."

"Oooh. Oh, gosh, that would be embarrassing as a teenager. But at least your parents are still together. It wasn't a wham-bam."

"Whoa." Axl put up his hand. "Can we just move on? I do not want to think about my parents having spontaneous sex."

Leighton shrugged. "I don't know. I think it's nice to know my parents have passion. Obviously, I don't want details but I love that they still flirt with each other. It's...reassuring."

That was an interesting response. "Reassuring of what?"

"That they love each other. But also that passion isn't solely for the young. Don't you want to know you'll still have passion when you're eighty? Like Bill and Soon-ja?"

Every time he tried to keep the conversation casual

Leighton seemed to steer it into something serious. The future. She was the kind of woman who wanted a commitment.

And he actually wished for a brief second that he could give it to her. Full on, marriage and the house and the boat and the dog and the kids.

"I don't think I'll ever stop wanting sex," he said, purposely missing the point. "I certainly want it right now."

She could have pressed, but she let him change the subject. "I am not having sex with you on this boat in front of a hundred buildings."

"There is always below deck."

She was considering it, he could tell. Axl moved closer to her, pulling her sunglasses off her face so he could see her eyes. "It will warm you up," he murmured.

"That sounds like man logic."

"Let me show you." Axl ran his hand over her thigh, up to where he could brush over the front of her shorts.

Suddenly, her phone started squawking. She jumped back and dug in her pocket. "That's my alert. Oh, my God, what did I forget?"

Axl sighed. Blue balls on the lake for him. He could just tell she wasn't in the sex zone. She was distracted by plans and parents and future dogs.

"Darn it! I totally forgot I have a staff meeting in thirty minutes. Axl, we have to go back."

He could have argued with her. Used all his sexual powers of persuasion, but he decided to let it go. Leighton was right. He had started all of this. Now his job was to make sure Leighton didn't lose her mind in the process of pulling out a fake wedding on five days notice. They worked really well as a team, something he wasn't used to, but had to admit he liked. They brought out the best in each other, complemented each other. It was more enjoyable than he ever could have imagined.

"Hang on," he told her. "I'll have you back in ten minutes."

But he did give her a kiss, hard, and cupped her sex through her shorts.

"I'm glad you drive too fast," he told her truthfully and stood up to start the boat.

"I wasn't speeding," Leighton said. "You just drive too slow in Minnesota."

"Maybe I should call you Speed Demon instead of 'babe.'"

"Maybe you shouldn't. Maybe you should just call me Leighton." She gave him a sweet smile.

Maybe what he wanted was to call her his.

CLEAVAGE.

Leighton laughed when she read the text from Axl as she stood in the dressing room of a local bridal shop the next day.

NO.

"What's so funny, sweetie?" the bridal attendant, whose name was June, asked her.

"My fiancé wants my dress to have cleavage."

June, who was in her sixties and wore a perpetual frown, shook her head. "Men are pigs."

Leighton was starting to think her mother had been right. She had wanted to have a gown flown in from LA but Leighton had thought it would be good PR to use a local shop. But June, the bridal shop employee, was the equivalent of the weather pattern they called June Gloom in LA. Cold and completely lacking in sunshine. This woman just didn't appear to enjoy her job because she had a serious attitude.

She also seemed to be a man hater.

Which was a buzz kill even for a fake wedding.

Leighton wished she had a friend with her.

But in a way, she did. Axl had been texting her nonstop.

He thought that he really was deserving of the stupid Ice Man nickname, but he wasn't. He was funny in a very dry way.

Send me a pic.

Leighton amused herself by sending him a picture of June, picking through the racks.

Axl sent her back an emoji with its tongue sticking out.

She laughed again.

June shot her an annoyed look over her shoulder. Leighton had yet to even try a gown on, she'd been there all of six minutes, and June clearly wanted her to disappear. It was time to take charge of the appointment.

She was good at making quick decisions and sorting through bullshit to get results. It was her job. She came by her nickname honestly. Taking a selfie blowing a kiss, she sent it to Axl. He texted back immediately.

You are so cute.

It gave her butterflies. Fucking butterflies.

"Where are your sweetheart necklines on a mermaid gown?" If Axl wanted cleavage, he was getting cleavage.

June looked at her blankly.

Determined not to be annoyed, she gave her a smile. "I'll just look around."

She knew her way around a bridal shop. Usually dresses were grouped by designer then displayed by style, but this shop seemed to have just unpacked stock and stuck it anywhere on the racks. Maybe there wasn't a high demand for wedding gowns in Beaver Bend. That seemed unlikely but she had no data. This just wasn't standard operating procedure in her experience.

After twenty minutes of pushing and shoving at dresses on the racks to see each dress, she realized two things. One, she needed to take her fitness more seriously because her arms were killing her. Two, this was an epic fail. Nothing was current or in style.

It left her wondering what the hell local brides did. Order online? Probably. Which could work except that left a woman no ability to try on a multitude of gowns and make her choice.

Super frustrating.

Leighton blew her hair out of her eyes. "June, thanks for your help but I'm not seeing anything here that works for me."

The woman turned and shot her a look like she was the biggest bitch on the planet. "You're not even going to try anything on?"

"No, thank you."

"I just spent thirty minutes pulling gowns," June said, her tone accusatory.

Leighton was taken aback. "Well, sorry, but I don't like any of these."

"Not rich enough for you, huh? No skin off my back, honey."

"Uh, I should think not." Stunned, Leighton grabbed her purse and left the store. She took a deep breath and felt a moment of pity for all the hopeful brides to step into this shop past, present, and future, and then started toward her rental car.

"Call Mom," she told her phone.

"Hi, baby! How's it going? What can Mommy do to help?"

Leighton realized she was about to make all her mother's dreams come true. "Mom, I need you to find me a dress today and overnight it so I can get fitted tomorrow. I can't find anything here."

"Well, good Lord, of course not. You're practically in the wilderness."

"Now that is an exaggeration. But there's just one bridal salon in town and the lady is a cranky-pants with a dated selection. So..." She took a deep breath. "I'm giving you free rein.

Pick out whatever you want." She was crunched for time, but also, curious what her mother would come up with.

"Whatever I want?" Her mother sounded like a kid in the candy store with a hundred dollar bill in hand.

"Whatever you want." Leighton propped her phone on her shoulder so she could root around in her handbag for sunglasses. It was chilly for summer but it was sunny. She couldn't see a darn thing. "Just one caveat, Mom."

"Poop. What?"

That made her laugh. "No, you'll like this. Axl requested cleavage so make sure the neckline isn't too demure."

"Sexy is my specialty."

Truer words were never spoken.

"But I'm stunned you're okay with that, Lele." Her mother did sound thoroughly shocked. "Maybe there is some of me in you after all."

That made her roll her eyes as she found her sunglasses and tried to yank them out of the handbag. "Doubtful. But I have to admit, I want to wow him. I want him to drool." She did. Real or not, she wanted that man's jaw to drop when he saw her on Saturday. "He seems to think I'm sexy, so I want to give him a great view."

"Drooling. Check. Let Mommy handle everything. He'll be eating out of your hand."

She'd rather he just eat her, but she kept her dirty thoughts to herself. "I totally trust you. Let me know what's going on. It's still mid-morning there so hopefully you can find something soon. I really want a dress here by tomorrow."

"I'm sure that won't be a problem."

It wouldn't. Money moved mountains and both of her parents were expert at using that to their advantage. Normally it made Leighton uncomfortable but right now she didn't have much choice. "Thanks, Mom. Call me later, but I'll see you tomorrow."

"Yay!"

"Yay" Leighton parroted because it would make her mother happy to sound over-the-moon excited. She was tugging out her sunglasses and attempting to end the call simultaneously when she dropped her phone.

It landed on the sidewalk but thankfully she didn't shatter the screen. When she rose again, she stuck her glasses on her face and her phone in her purse. She realized Winnie Schwartz was standing in the doorway to her groomer's shop, smoking a cigarette.

"Hi, Winnie," she said, waving.

"Hey."

Since her first contact with Winnie the woman had never been anything but bubbly and sweet. Now she looked and sounded sullen. She was leaning against the wall, ankles crossed.

"Are you excited for Saturday?"

Winnie took a hit off her cigarette. "Cut the crap, Leighton. I know you're getting married Saturday too. And thanks to you, no one has the time of day for me. I might as well have eloped. Everyone all over town is talking about you and Axl and how it was love at first sight."

The venom in Winnie's voice shocked her. First June had been sulky, now Winnie was angry. It wasn't often that Leighton drew the ire of other women. She wasn't someone who had ever inspired jealousy, at least not in Beverly Hills. "I'm sorry, Winnie. I didn't think that it would cause any issues for you." That wasn't entirely true. She hadn't really given much thought to Winnie at all. She had been worried about saving her own ass.

Winnie shrugged. "It's whatever. I guess it's my fault. I

applied to the show without talking to Todd and he never wanted to do it. I'm just sorry that I won in the first place. And sorry that you thought it was okay to steal my special day."

With that, as Leighton stood with her mouth wide open, Winnie tossed her cigarette on the ground, stomped on it, and kicked open the door to her shop.

Leighton stood there, feeling as kicked as that door.

If she was in love with Axl, she wouldn't feel guilty. Winnie was right. She shouldn't have applied to be on the show without her fiancé's approval or knowledge. But because this wasn't a real marriage and was just the two of them trying to save their own respective butts, she did feel a twinge of something that felt a lot like guilt.

It would suck to be the bride who had a wedding on the same day as a whole town was buzzing about a TV wedding. Especially since it involved one of their own men in blue.

Not wanting Winnie to come back out and drive her point home harder, Leighton unlocked her rental and climbed in. She needed to regroup, put it behind her, and go meet the tent guy. Yet she had a pit in her stomach and a telltale scratchy throat that indicated anxiety. God, she hated that sensation. Feeling like she couldn't breathe, she hit the button to send the window down and sucked in some fresh air.

Her phone buzzed with a text notification.

Axl.

You okay?

How did he always know when she was vulnerable?

It was like he had a sixth sense.

Dress shopping was a failure. I'm going to have to have my mother send me something.

In three days?

My mother will have it to me by tomorrow.

Axl's face popped up on her screen. He was actually calling

her.

"Hello?"

"What else it wrong? You don't sound right."

Now how in the hell did he know she didn't "sound right" in a text message? The man was psychic.

Either that or they had a legitimate connection.

Which she was starting to think they did.

"I ran into Winnie Schwartz and she said I stole her wedding day."

There was a pause. "But didn't her fiancé cancel their appearance on the show?"

"Yes."

"Then she should be pissed at him, not you. Or hell, maybe not pissed at all. What's the big deal? It's not like we have the same guest list and they chose us over them."

Men didn't get it. They didn't understand that a wedding day was life to a woman. That she waited since childhood to be the star of the show for approximately twelve hours. To know that while your wedding was going on, another woman was having a splashy wedding for TV across town would be upsetting. She totally understood that.

"I think she's just disappointed. I can relate to that. It's a big deal."

"So you feel bad for her?"

"Yes."

"You're a nicer person than me. I think this is on her. Or her fiancé. I wouldn't worry about it. But I think you're very sweet to care."

Leighton took a deep breath. "I still feel bad, but thank you. I'll see you tomorrow?"

She wished she could see him that night but honestly, she had so much to do and he worked until eleven. She wasn't sure she could keep her eyes open until then, let alone fool around.

It pained her to say it but she needed sleep more than an orgasm.

"Tomorrow? Are you serious? I can't see you tonight?"

He sounded so salty about it she was touched. "You work late and I am going to be so tired. I can't face the parents tomorrow without a good night's sleep."

"I understand, baby. But I want to sleep next to you."

He sounded a little pouty and Leighton thought it was adorable. So much for being the self-proclaimed loner. "You'll be okay, I'm sure."

"Leave me a key at the front desk and I'll just slip in and get in bed with you. I promise I won't wake you up."

Damn him for being adorable on top of being sexy and ridiculously masculine. It was a trio of traits she could not resist. She crumpled like a tissue. "If that's what you want."

"I want."

There it was again. The distinct sensation in her chest of her catching feelings. "If I wake up with you trying to get in my pants I'm going to be upset with you."

Axl laughed softly. "That is the biggest lie I've ever heard."

Damn it. He was right.

ELEVEN

AXL KNEW he was being ridiculous. It was stupid as fuck to be going over to Leighton's hotel room just so he could rest his hand on her hip while they both slept. Never had he been the guy who needed to share a bed with someone.

In fact, just the opposite.

But there was something about the fact that there was an expiration date on their relationship that made him want to steal every moment he could with her. With any other woman he had dated this would have never occurred to him. His unwillingness to see one girlfriend after his work shifts had actually resulted in their breaking up. She felt unimportant. He felt annoyed.

The desk clerk didn't seem at all alarmed that he was at the desk asking for a key to Leighton's room. He would have been concerned by that except the woman said, "I can't wait to watch your wedding on TV, officer." She was in her early twenties and she handed him the key with a bright smile.

That took him aback. Sometimes he forgot this whole thing was going to be watched by random people in their living rooms across the country. "Thank you. Hopefully I won't make an ass out of myself."

She laughed riotously, like he was downright hilarious.

"Thanks for the key. I don't want to wake Leighton up."

She laughed again and nodded enthusiastically.

Never having been considered a funny guy, he wasn't sure how to react to her laughter other than to nod back and shake the key card in the air. "Goodnight."

Her response was yet again a peel of laughter. Axl had to get the hell out of there. He found it was the same kind of reaction doing the strip event had created. Not his style, that was for sure. He didn't crave attention. Not that way.

Gingerly he opened the door to Leighton's room and stepped inside. It was not easy to divest himself of a gun, cuffs, car keys, his wallet, and entire uniform quietly but he thought he did a reasonable enough job. He could hear Leighton's steady breathing in the dark room. She had the blackout drapes tightly drawn and he couldn't see a damn thing. In his underwear he moved slowly, trying to remember exactly where the furniture was placed in the room.

He bumped the edge of the bed, his eyes adjusting a little. He could see Leighton's blonde hair spread across the pillow, lying on her side. She was a bed hog. It was a king-size bed and she was dead center. Easing the bedspread back, he slid in beside her. He couldn't resist the urge to spoon her. Leighton had the best ass. Awesome tits too. She smelled like shampoo and has he settled in beside her, the soft feel of her warm ass cheeks beneath her soft cotton nightgown, he couldn't help it. He started to get a hard-on.

Instead of shifting away from her he was a greedy bastard who snaked his hand around her front and cupped her breast. It was a dick move, he knew that. But she was way too tempting. He realized Leighton wasn't full asleep, though, because damned if she didn't wiggle that sweet ass up against his cock.

"Is that a gun or are you just happy to see me?" she murmured, sounding sleepy.

"What do you think?"

"I think you're a very bad man."

"Can't argue with that." He teased her nipple, which drew a tiny gasp from her. "You don't have to do anything. I'll do all the work."

"Axl..." It wasn't a protest. More like a moan.

"That's my name."

Her ass bumped him again. "Make me come."

"I thought you wanted to sleep." Axl shifted her hair and kissed the back of her neck.

"It will only take a minute."

That made him laugh softly. "Whatever you want, sweetheart."

He eased his fingers into her panties and started to stroke across her clit, and inside her. Leighton responded immediately, with soft sounds of approval and her body growing damp for him. She rocked her hips so that his finger went deeper inside her.

She was right. It only took a minute before she was shuddering in pleasure.

Damn, he needed to make a note to himself. Sleepy Leighton came fast and hard.

Probably because she was relaxed. That wasn't always the case when she was wide awake.

"Yum," she murmured.

"I agree. Turn towards me, baby."

He had to encourage her but she rolled onto her opposite side, languid and sleepy-eyed. He got rid of his boxer briefs, lifted her leg onto his hip, and eased into her warm heat. She moaned and he thought there was nothing better than this. Her slick hot pussy, the scent of her arousal, the sound of her voice enjoying his cock.

Now he knew why he had come here tonight. This was it. Tomorrow her family arrived and everything went full throttle.

Their last stolen moments alone, with any sort of truth or intimacy between them was right here, right now. His eyes trained on hers, her fingers stroking across his chest. Her nightgown bunched at her waist while he slowly, methodically, thrust his cock inside her body.

He thought it was so fucking hot that she wore a nightgown. Every other woman he'd dated slept in oversized T-shirts and basketball shorts or pajama pants.

Not Leighton. She was like his little piece of old Hollywood, curvy and silky and sexy.

When Axl felt Leighton orgasm a second time, he joined her. Let himself explode inside her while he gripped her hip.

He wanted to say something. He didn't know what. But within a minute or two of his coming, Leighton was already drifting back into sleep. His cock still inside her.

So he brushed her hair back off her forehead and watched her eyes flutter and her mouth drift open as she settled into a deeper breathing.

He didn't think he would be able to sleep. He never crashed right after a three to eleven shift. But he did.

His last conscious thought was that he just might be falling love with Leighton.

"WHAT IS ACTUALLY HAPPENING?" Axl murmured to Leighton. He was sitting at his parents' dining room table next to Leighton, his arm over the back of her chair.

"I'm not sure," she whispered back. "This is very weird."

His parents and Leighton's parents hadn't eyeballed each

other suspiciously or been confrontational in any way. They had hit it off faster than couples on a reality dating show. Axl had been concerned that the mothers might be aloof but they were slinging back wine and laughing like they had known each other for forty years. His father and Dieter were deep in a discussion on Bitcoin.

No one was paying any attention to either him or Leighton.

Which was fine with him but it was still strange nonetheless.

His parents' house was an eighties colonial that had undergone a refresh in the kitchen and bathrooms in the last ten years but the dining room was still the way it had been when he was a kid. Dark burgundy walls and a deep mahogany table and hutch. Axl had thought he mother would be worried about her décor the way she was about her hair, but neither of those seemed to be on her mind at all. She and Barbie were discussing the merits of pedicures with fish, whatever the hell that was.

Barbie was vivacious and over-the-top. He could see how she would be the life of the party, but like Leighton, she had a way of making everyone around her feel comfortable. Leighton seemed to have her father's personality. Quiet, thoughtful, organized.

"May I have another of those sashimi rolls?" Dieter asked, pointing to the platter in the center of the table.

"Of course," his mother said.

The decision had been made to order food given that it was last minute and his mother had rather belligerently chosen sushi because the Van Burens were from California.

But to her surprise, she had enjoyed it herself, which Axl found ironic.

"What do we do?" Axl asked Leighton under his breath. "I feel like we could leave and they would never notice."

"I feel like I'm in an alternate reality." Leighton turned to him, amused. "I guess it's a good thing, right?"

Sure, if they were a real couple.

Which it kind of felt like they were. Which freaked him the fuck out.

"Better than a food fight."

But then Leighton's father, over coffee, said, "If you two want me to glance over the prenuptial agreement, I'd be happy to take a look."

Shit.

That had never occurred to Axl. Of course Leighton's family would want a prenup. They had a ton of money. And, also predictably, his mother was offended.

"Why, do you think Axl might be trying to take advantage of Leighton?"

If this were a real marriage, Axl would sign a prenuptial agreement. But it wasn't, so it hadn't entered his head. They had some guy Leighton had hired marrying them without actually getting a marriage license. Nothing would be legal. "Mom, it's fine. I don't think they were suggesting that at all."

"No, no, of course not," Dieter said. "It's for both of them. It's standard. You wouldn't want Leighton to inherit *your* property if something happened, would you? Contracts just take out the negative emotion and allow the room for all the joy, yes?"

Amazingly, it placated his mother. "I suppose," she said reluctantly.

"I can sign whatever you want," Axl told Leighton.

Her lips were pursed. "I think we should talk about this later."

"How much later?" Axl's father asked. "The wedding is in two days."

Yes. It was.

It scared the absolute shit out of him because something was not right in his head. He wanted to spend more time with Leighton. No, he absolutely did not want to get married for real. But he wouldn't mind seeing her still after all of this and seeing if maybe, just maybe it could go somewhere. A real relationship. Which was impossible.

He stood up abruptly.

"What are you doing?" his mother asked, looking mortified at his complete lack of manners.

"I need a drink."

LEIGHTON WATCHED Axl disappear into the family room where the Moores had a bar. She gave a weak smile to everyone around the table and shrugged. Her palms felt damp and she ran them down the front of her floral dress.

It was making her uncomfortable that everyone seemed to be getting along. While the thought of animosity had been scary, it wouldn't have felt so intimate then. This felt far too close to real to be anything other than horrifying.

Axl seemed to be having the same response since he was headed straight for the booze. She'd only known him six days but he didn't seem to be much of a drinker. He'd said so himself and his lack of home liquor led her to believe that was true. His parents had a full bar, though, and she heard bottles clinking around as if he were searching for something.

"I think this is all a little overwhelming," she said weakly.

"Well, that's what happens when you rush these things," Hillary said. It was evident she thought they both deserved some stress for being so impulsive.

"Oh, pooh," her own mother said. "Marriage is always going to be overwhelming. Sometimes you just have to dive in."

"You know what they say. The secret to a successful marriage is still a secret," her father said.

"Dad!" Leighton almost laughed. "That's not advice. That's like a George Burns punch line."

Axl came back to the table with something that looked like bourbon. Poured very high in the glass.

Her father shrugged. "Just respect your marriage, you two, and everything will be fine."

That was about as unsettling as Winnie's words that Leighton was stealing her day.

They weren't respecting anything.

She swallowed hard. Marriage wasn't a TV show. Marriage wasn't something to be flippant about. Marriage was Soon-ja leaving her family and her home behind because of love. Marriage was her own father willing to accept digs about their age difference because he loved his wife. Marriage was Axl's mother and father raising three kids and still enjoying each other's company after a crazy night at a Guns N' Roses concert.

She wanted that. All of that. She wanted a man to look at her for years and years with love still shining in his eyes. She wanted a man who would defend her when her mother took a dig at her weight and who made her feel beautiful, just the way she was.

And she wanted it with Axl.

It was happening. She could feel it. Her throat was closing up and her heart started to race.

No one seemed to notice so she concentrated on breathing through her nose. God, she hated this. It made her feel so weak to not be able to control her anxiety. Everyone always just thought she was overreacting or that she could control it. But it was physical, an actual wave of predictable symptoms that crashed over her until she felt like she was having a heart attack or that she couldn't breathe. Even when she knew intellectually she wasn't going to die, it really, in those moments, felt like it.

But then there was Axl, his hand on her leg, squeezing. His

voice murmuring in her ear, "It's okay. You're okay." His hand, lifting his glass to her lips and encouraging her to take a sip.

Her vision had blurred but with his help and repeated soft words, he returned her to clarity. She could hear her mother saying, "Oh, shit, she's doing it again, Dieter. Do something."

"What's going on?" Hillary asked.

Leighton was mortified. She was too embarrassed to look at Axl's parents so she focused on him. He cupped her cheeks, his thumbs massaging over her skin. "That's good. You're fine."

She didn't say anything. She could only imagine what people living in Northern Minnesota would think of her anxiety. Axl's parents seemed very salt-of-the-earth and when she shot a quick glance over at them, they looked horrified.

"Are you having a seizure?" Hillary asked.

"Panic attack," her own mother said. "She gets those a lot."

"Oh, dear. That's unfortunate."

Which to Leighton's ears might as well have been "so the bitch is broken." She had no clue what Hillary or Rob were actually thinking but it felt like something to be ashamed of because she had always despised her anxiety.

"It doesn't happen a lot anymore," she said, feeling defensive.

And as grateful as she was for Axl's support, she saw in his eyes that he didn't agree with her assessment that it didn't happen frequently. He was right. She'd done this three times since she'd met him.

"It doesn't matter if it does or it doesn't. What matters is that you're okay." He kissed her forehead and dropped his arms back down.

"Oh, my goodness, you have such a good touch with her," her mother said. "They usually last longer than that."

They did. But Axl was a big, strong, calming force for her. An anchor.

Axl gave her a smile that made her toes curl. "Leighton has a good touch with me, too."

She sighed, loving how he always made her feel like his equal. Like she had something to contribute. Without even thinking about it, she reached for his hand and laced her fingers through his.

"Well. Who wants coffee and dessert?" Hillary said, swiftly, like it was important to move on. Or maybe because their intimacy was upsetting to her.

Leighton wasn't sure if that made her feel better or worse.

"You should see Leighton's dress," her mother said cheerfully. "It will knock your socks off, Axl!"

Leighton had seen it and was pleasantly surprised that her mother had chosen a dress that reflected her personality. It was certainly blingy, but not outrageous the way she had been expecting. It was mermaid style, which was what she would have chosen for herself. She had felt good in it when she had tried it on and it only needed minor modifications. The veil hadn't arrived yet but was due in tomorrow. It made her feel like maybe her mother did understand her, and did respect who she was as a person.

"Is it low cut?" Axl asked. "That's all I care about."

His mother reached across the table and slapped his arm. "Knock it off. This is your future mother-in-law. Show some respect."

"It is low cut!" her mother said, not sounding the least bit offended.

Leighton reached out for Axl's glass and took a giant sip, fighting back the urge to choke.

It settled on her hard and fast that this wasn't worth her job. This was torture. Glorious, delicious, horrible torture. It was like having everything you'd ever wanted knowing it was all going away in a matter of days. It felt real, but it was fake. It was an emotional tornado and Axl sat there though it, the eye. Calm. Unperturbed, while she was spinning around unable to grab onto anything but him.

She didn't want to say it was a mistake, but God, she had enjoyed being with Axl so much. But she didn't like the lie.

"I can't wait to see her," Axl said.

It was like being on a reality TV show where everyone else had a script but her.

Axl was doing this to save his ass. She needed to remember that.

She may be falling in love, but he wasn't.

Oh, God, she was falling in love.

Damn it.

She took another sip and prayed she would not make an ass out of herself by telling him how she felt. Because he wasn't going to fall in love with her even if she had all the wedding lingerie in the state of Minnesota.

TWELVE

"I CAN'T BELIEVE you want to play poker for your bachelor party," Sullivan complained. "I wanted to go to the strip club."

"It's not a real bachelor party," he reminded him. They were in the back room at Tap That. Sullivan's dad and two young bartenders in their twenties were running the bar.

"So, I came here from Chicago for a fake wedding. Fantastic," Brandon said, shaking his head.

"I told you that you didn't have to come. I was honest about what's going on here."

"No one else knows it's fake. So if I don't show it would make me look like the shittiest friend ever. People would be like that fucking guy can't even make his best friend's wedding. What a dick."

"You are a dick."

Brandon threw his cards down. "I'm out. For the record, you owe me a plane ticket. I was just here last weekend."

"You make like five times what I do. Fuck off." Regardless of the reason, he was glad to see Brandon twice in a short period of time. He was also glad to see he had a full house in his hand. He slid a twenty in the center of the table.

"Ten times, more likely," Brandon said, with a grin.

"It doesn't matter if this is real or not," Sullivan insisted. "It's a perfect excuse to go to the strip club and no one can give us crap for it."

Rick tossed a handful of chips in his mouth. "I don't want to go to the strip club. There's only one woman I want to see naked and that's Sloane."

"Yeah, my sister, you asshole. Thanks for that visual."

"Your sister is hot. Get over it."

Sullivan sipped his whiskey. "Me: Don't have sex with my sister. Rick: whips his dick out and falls on her five minutes later."

"That's a lie. It was *her* idea that first night, if you want the truth."

Sullivan grimaced. "No, I don't want the truth. I want nothing to do with your sex life with my sister."

"Can we all talk about my sex life?" Jesse asked. "Because it's fucking awesome."

That made Axl laugh. "No. Let's talk about the Vikings. I'd rather argue with you guys about football than women."

Sloane popped her head into the back room. "Uh, guys, I need to talk to you."

"Get out," Sullivan said. "You're not allowed in here."

Sloane rolled her eyes at her brother. "Whatever, loser. My dad owns half this bar, you know. But anyway, there is kind of a commotion out here. Leighton and her friends have arrived."

That made Axl look over at her in alarm. "So?" Leighton wasn't a party girl. He didn't think. She hadn't mentioned she'd be coming to Tap That but it wasn't surprising. It was the largest pub in town.

"There are a bunch of guys hitting on her friends. And maybe her."

"Are her friends hot?" Jesse asked.

"I don't know. I guess." Sloane shrugged. "But Leighton looks uncomfortable so I thought Axl might want to know."

Axl figured if Sloane thought it was worth mentioning than it wasn't just some random guy offering to buy her a drink. He stood up. "Nobody look at my hand."

What he saw when he went out into the bar had him grinning instead of concerned. Leighton was sitting at a table reading a book. She was sipping a glass of wine. As if she were at home in her apartment instead of in the midst of her bachelorette "party." There was a group of people he didn't recognize right behind her. The women were thin and tan and strangers to him, presumably her California friends. He recognized the men ogling them as locals.

Jackson, the cameraman, was sitting next to Leighton looking annoyed.

"Hey," Axl said, coming up behind her and massaging her shoulders. "What are you doing here? And why are you reading a book in a bar."

She looked up. "Hi. My friends wanted to see a local bar so I wanted to make them happy but I'm exhausted. Whenever I'm beat down I turn to Jane Austen. Comfort reads."

He kept rubbing her shoulders. He didn't doubt that she was exhausted. She had been going nonstop for six days. "You know what I want?" he murmured, bending over to speak straight into her ear.

"What?"

"I want to throw you over my shoulder, take you home, and spend the night in bed." He liked his friends but he saw them all the time. And they didn't have bodies like Leighton.

She shook her head. "That's not going to happen, though I doubt I would have the energy for it anyway. I have about two minutes before they realize I'm not doing a shot and come over to drag me to the bar. Oh, and Jackson wants to do an interview."

Axl eyed Jackson, who looked glum. "Do we really have to do an interview?" Axl asked him, giving him a stern look he hoped would intimidate him into backing down. Jackson didn't look thrilled about any of this so maybe he could talk him out of it. "Leighton is tired."

"We really should, unfortunately." Jackson sipped a craft beer. "Can you believe it was just a week ago we were here for Winnie's bachelorette party? It feels like I've been in this town a thousand years."

Seven days. That was kind of crazy to think about. It felt both like he'd known Leighton for a while and yet like he'd blinked and this week had disappeared.

"I actually owe you, Jackson. If you hadn't made that comment to Leighton about me we might not be standing here right now."

"Fabulous."

A guy who was in Leighton's group of friends at the bar came over and slid into an empty chair, fanning himself. He was dressed in a button-up shirt. "Leighton, is this Officer Hottie?"

"Zach, this is Axl. Axl, my best friend, Zach."

Axl stuck his hand out. "Nice to meet you."

"My pleasure. I've heard so much about you." He lifted his hands to indicate what Axl had to assume was dick size. "So much."

That actually made him laugh.

"Oh, my God, stop! I did not." Leighton put her book in her purse. "You just love to embarrass me, Zach."

"It's not really that hard to make you squirm." He turned to Jackson. "And what's your name? I would like to know since you're my future ex-husband."

Jackson looked like he would rather do thirty days in San

Quentin. "I'm the cameraman for *Wedding Crashers*. That's probably all you need to know."

"Rude." Zach took a sip of his drink and waved his hand to Axl. "Sit down. Join us. Though why are you crashing Leighton's bachelorette party?"

"Technically, she crashed mine. My friends and I are playing poker in the back room."

"Scandalous."

"Not really."

"Oh, that's not a euphemism for something dirty?"

Axl laughed. "No. Not even close. We really are just playing poker."

There was a high-pitched yell from the bar.

"My friends aren't usually this loud," Leighton said. "But I think the long flight and the fresh air have whipped them up."

"You should introduce me. And I see my friend Jesse is already hitting on your friends. Surprise, surprise."

"My friend Sandra's father owns a professional hockey team. They probably have a lot in common." Leighton stood up, like she was resigned to all of this, but was not intending to enjoy it.

He met her three girlfriends in a blur of waves and greetings and "Oh, Leighton, he's fucking hot!" while he tried to picture how Leighton fit into this particular group. She was definitely the quiet one. Though he wouldn't call her shy, despite the fact she had said she was.

She was *him* in his friend group. They were both the hang-back-and-observe members of their respective crowds. Brandon had now joined Jesse and they were chatting up Sandra, Christina, and Jordan. "Should we do our interview now and get it over with?" he asked Leighton. "We're not needed here."

She shot him a rueful look. "Clearly."

Jackson seemed to have warmed up to Zach. They were

bent over talking. Despite the dirty look she got from Zach, Leighton interrupted.

"Jackson, let's get this interview over with."

"You're kind of a bridezilla," he told her. "You have been cranky this week."

Leighton's mouth dropped. "I have not. I'm just busy."

"Let's just do the filming," Axl said to Jackson. "So you can go back to your hotel."

And he could talk Leighton into going home with him.

"Fine. Let's go outside. It's too loud in here."

They were standing in front of the bar under the flashing fluorescent Tap That sign. It made Axl grin. He didn't think either Jackson or Leighton noticed so maybe he was just a fucking pervert but he thought it was hilarious. But him being a dirt bag was not what was needed for the damn show.

After Jackson got his camera up and ready he started to ask them questions. "Are you ready to get married?"

"Yes." He knew he was supposed to elaborate on that but even if they really were getting married he wasn't sure he would have anything else to say. That wasn't his style.

"I'm sure something will go wrong tomorrow because it always does," Leighton said, mostly looking at the sidewalk in front of the bar. "But we'll just roll with it."

Neither one of them really answered that the way they were supposed to and Jackson sighed. "Tell me what you love about Leighton."

Leighton's head snapped up. "I didn't put that question in there, Jackson. What the heck?"

Axl was taken aback too, but what the hell, of course that would be a question if any of this were real. He was amused that Leighton was outraged but still couldn't bring herself to swear. She only seemed to cuss when she either wanted sex or they were having sex. He found that hot.

Their fingers were entwined, something he didn't do very often. He wasn't really a hand-holding guy. But Leighton always seemed so delicate to him. It felt natural to touch each other this intimately. He lifted their hands now and spoke to the camera.

"We're a good fit," he said. He meant that. They'd had a good week. It wasn't a lie. It was a week he would remember fondly for the rest of his life. God, fondly. That was such a fucking understatement. He sounded like his mother when she referred to being fond of coffee. This was something else entirely. This had been the fastest and hardest he had fallen for any woman ever and he *cherished* the time together.

So he turned to speak directly to Leighton. He wanted her to know that while this was not a real engagement, he had enjoyed being with her. Getting to know her. "Leighton is special. She has a huge heart and a consideration for others. The first minute I laid eyes on her I knew she was different."

"In what way?" Jackson asked.

Axl squeezed her hand and stared into her green eyes. "She's perfect and she has no idea that she is. She's intelligent, generous, and amazing at her job. She's as soft and delicate as the roses she loves, yet she has an inner strength I don't think she even knows she possesses. And I've enjoyed every minute of this week with her, falling for her."

Leighton bit her lip and without warning there were tears in her eyes. Axl felt it again, that strange protective surge he had around her. He reached up and wiped her eye before the tear fell down her cheek.

"And Leighton, what do you love about Axl?"

"He's a nurturer," she said, which kneed him in the gut.

That was the first thing she said about him? It brought up emotions he hadn't even known he was capable of.

"And he's thoughtful and smart and loyal."

Axl was overwhelmed and he couldn't resist. He bent down and kissed her, taking her mouth in a deep passionate kiss that he hoped conveyed everything he felt without having to say it. That she deserved a lifetime of happiness with a house and children and a rose garden of her own.

That he wanted to be like Bill, and throw caution to the fucking wind and marry her and get her a puppy, but that he couldn't because his heart was frozen as solid as the lake in February and not even her sunny California smile could thaw it. Not entirely. Not the way she deserved.

So, he kissed her and willed her to feel it, to understand him, to know that she was something really fucking special.

When he pulled back, he needed to leave. He couldn't look at her and keep his shit together. "We're done here," he told Jackson. "Go get some rest." He squeezed Leighton's hand and dropped it. "Come on. I'll take you back to your friends. Enjoy your girl time."

"I thought you wanted to throw me over your shoulder and kidnap me?" she said, sounding a little hopeful.

He wanted to do a lot of things. None of them were smart. "At least once this week I need to resist my impulses." He led her to the door of the bar and yanked it open for her. "I will see you tomorrow, sweetheart."

"Yeah. Right." Leighton shot him a look he couldn't interpret then marched over to the bar.

He watched her do a shot with her girlfriends before he made his way back to his poker game.

He lost his fucking shirt to Sullivan that night.

Because he was one hundred percent distracted by thoughts of a sweet blonde who looked at him like she could fall in love with him.

And he wanted her to.

• • •

"ZACH, I'm so screwed. I'm just so completely and totally screwed." Leighton paced back and forth in her hotel room. Her mother was texting her asking about the bachelorette night and if she'd had fun and she couldn't bring herself to answer.

Fun wasn't the way to describe it. Knocked on her ass was a better descriptive.

"Okay, calm down. What's going on?" Zach looked at himself in the mirror. "This lighting sucks. Where are you getting ready tomorrow? Because this room is not going to cut it. I can't do your makeup in these conditions."

"I don't care about the lighting. What I care about is that we have a problem. Or rather, I have a problem."

"What's that? If Sandra is currently having sex with the hockey guy, it's not a big deal. She likes to get her ho on when she's out of town. She'll be on time tomorrow, no worries."

Leighton didn't care who her friends had sex with. "Don't call her a ho. That is not nice. A woman is allowed to have fun."

"Got it. As if I would ever judge anyone for multiple sex partners. Including at the same time."

He was missing the point. What she cared about was who *she* was having sex with. Axl. "I'm in love with Axl!" She paused and held her hand to her chest at the very words being spoken out loud. Everything inside her just melted at the thought of him.

To her it seemed the words hung in the air, like she'd grabbed a bullhorn and set it off along with the most outrageous statement ever made.

Zach did not agree. He looked one hundred percent blasé. "Well, duh. We knew that was going to happen."

For a second, she was stunned.

Then she realized he had a good point. "What am I supposed to do now?" Leighton sighed as she remembered what he'd said to her in that interview outside of Tap That. "He's just so... everything. He's romantic and sexy and strong and caring and..."

Zach stood up straight and eyed her. "Am I going to have to slap you? That's usually what happens at this point. Or throw a drink in your face."

"Why the hell would you throw a drink in my face?" she asked, peeling her sweater off and throwing it on the dresser. She was burning up for no apparent reason. "I think we can skip that step."

"To talk sense into you." Zach reached out for her.

Leighton dodged him, alarmed. "Don't you dare shake or slap me. I'm not that hysterical."

"I was going to hug you, I swear."

Not sure she should trust him, she let him draw her into his arms. It was actually a genuine, reassuring hug. "What do I do?" she asked him again.

"You get fake married tomorrow and have amazing wedding night sex. Then, you lay your heart on the line and see what happens."

"I can't do that!" Axl had made it clear he was in this short term, nothing more.

"Then you get fake married, have great wedding sex, fake break up and come home to LA with a happy vagina and move on with your life."

"I guess I could do that," she said, even though she felt grumpy about it. "Even though it sucks. But that is my only option, isn't it?"

"You could skip the wedding and the wedding night sex all together and do the fake breakup first."

"That sounds even less like what I want." She definitely wanted the sex. "I want one last night with Axl."

"Lies. You don't want one last night with him. You want indefinite nights with him."

"I do." She sighed.

Then she realized she was supposed to say those words the next day to his face and she looked at Zach. "Feel free to slap me now. I think I need it."

"I'm not going to slap you. I'm going to put you to bed so you can get some quality sleep. Then I'm going to do your hair and makeup in the morning and you're going to be so fucking hot that man will *wish* he could marry you for real."

It wasn't much of a plan but it was the only one she had. "And then what?"

"You break his heart before he breaks yours."

Probably too late for that. Hers felt pretty darn cracked.

THIRTEEN

LEIGHTON HADN'T SLEPT one lousy wink and the morning was a blur of coffee and robes and makeup and girlfriends and her mother delicately crying so as not to screw up her false eyelashes. She kept thinking about her parents, and Axl's parents, and Bill and Soon-ja and the sanctity of marriage.

Of the fact that on the other side of town, in a stone church, Winnie was marrying Todd, some of the wind taken out of her sails.

Bill's property was stunning. Her team had set up a gorgeous tent with floral chandeliers and boundless pink accents. Servers had handed guests a glass of champagne upon arrival. It was perfect. Exactly what she would want if she were really getting married.

Which she wasn't.

Yet she was standing in a gown that she freaking loved, if she were honest, and her grandmother's lace veil from Germany that her father had surprised her with. She'd had the very awkward moment where she had had to tell her father she did not want him to walk her down the aisle because it was essentially a single-file arch and aisle. The real reason being she didn't want to waste that special moment on a fake ceremony. If and when she did get married, she wanted to hang on to her father's arm and see his joy.

She thought, quite simply, she might throw up.

There were cameras everywhere, which further contributed to the feeling that this was just a big production. Which it was.

Yet the rose archway was in front of her and she was frozen. She could not bring herself to step through Soon-ja's flowers and into a greenhouse only to be a faker.

She stood there and stood there. She paced a little.

The music started twice. She could hear the guests starting to murmur and shuffle restlessly.

Forcing herself forward, she took three steps and spotted Axl at the front of the greenhouse. She froze again, actually bumping into Jackson, who had his camera in her face. He lowered it.

Are you okay? He mouthed.

She shook her head.

She turned, planning to retreat and get the heck out of there but there was staff and two cameramen crawling all over the entrance to the arch. Feeling trapped, like she was either going to descend into a full-blown panic attack or vomit in the grass, she did the only thing she could.

Leighton lifted her skirt and took off up the aisle.

STANDING at the makeshift altar waiting for Leighton was the scariest thing Axl had ever done besides combat. He was sweating bullets and feeling shit he had no business feeling.

"Are you okay?" Rick asked him, standing beside him. Rick stepped slightly in front of Axl to block him from the guests' watchful eyes. "You don't have to do this, buddy. I can spin a story while you slip out the front."

"I don't know what's going on with me, man," he told Rick. "But I feel like maybe there's more to this than I thought." He rubbed his jaw and said, "There's just something about Leighton. I just think... I don't know. I feel like I need to go talk to her."

To say what, he had no idea. But he needed to see her.

Rick's eyebrows shot up. "Dude, you're in love with her, aren't you?"

That took him aback. "What? No. Of course not." They'd known each other a week. It was ridiculous. He didn't fall in love that easily.

No one fell in love that easily. That was for movies and reality TV. Not life.

Yet when he glanced behind Rick and saw Leighton standing under the arch of roses, looking absolutely stunning from head to toe, he doubted everything he'd ever known about love and relationships and his future.

Holy shit, she was beautiful.

And if he wasn't in love with her now, he sure in the hell could be soon.

She was wearing a form-fitting dress that showed off all her curves to advantage, nipping in at the waist and hugging her hips. It was sparkling and bridal and yep, there was cleavage. All the cleavage in the world. The veil on her head made her look like an angel. A vision in white, surrounded by pink flowers.

His bride.

For a second he seriously could not breathe.

They weren't just playing with fire here, they were juggling with dynamite.

Because everything about this was so wrong and so right and so completely ass backwards that he didn't know how he could do this without talking to Leighton first and telling her everything that was running through his head.

He was about to start down the aisle to her, to say what, he had no idea.

But Leighton beat him to the punch. She picked up her skirt with one hand and started running. Stunned, he just watched her.

"What the hell is she doing?" Rick asked, bewildered.

The guests were all giving gasps and exclamations. Jackson was running after her, camera up, as were two other guys behind him left and right. Leighton ran up to him.

And right past him.

What the fuck was going on?

Axl reached out and grabbed Leighton by the arm, whirling her around. Panic was written all over her features.

"Sweetheart, what are you doing?" he asked, trying to pull her close to him. "Talk to me."

"I made a huge mistake," she whispered frantically. "This isn't me. I can't do this."

He knew exactly what she meant. He was feeling the same way. This wasn't them. All the cameras, the elegance, the fuss.

The fakeness.

Speaking of cameras, one popped up over his shoulder. He turned and glared at Jackson. "Get that out of my face or I'll break it."

"I need to get the shot."

Axl pushed the camera down so he could see Jackson's face. "Back the fuck off. Now."

When he turned back to Leighton she was breathing hard and swiping at her veil, which had dragged across her cheek. "I have to get out of here, Axl. Seriously."

"Are you saying you don't want to do this?" What shocked him was how much that made his heart drop into his gut.

"I want this to be real," Leighton said. She looked up at him with her heart in her eyes, and he saw his future. "Is this real?"

"No, it's not real." He opened his mouth to expound on that. To tell her that it could be real.

But Leighton gave a cry of dismay and ripped herself out of his grip. She ran out of the back of the greenhouse, jumping off the back ledge and twisting her ankle.

"Leighton!" He ran after her, scared. He didn't know where she thought she was going and he wanted a chance to talk to her. To explain.

"Holy shit," someone said from behind him.

"Do not follow them," he heard Rick order the cameraman.

A woman was wailing and trying to get through the crowd. A glance back showed it was Barbie dressed to the nines, slapping at her husband, who was keeping her from running after Leighton. "Let me go to my baby!"

It was chaos and drama and something he could honestly say he would have never thought he would be a part of in his entire lifetime.

Leaping off the stairs down into the grass he went after Leighton. She had thrown her veil off and abandoned her shoes so she could run faster, but she was wearing a skin-tight dress and it wasn't easy to move in that thing. He caught up with her within fifteen feet.

But when he went to grab her hand and stop her, she slapped at her. "Get away from me."

And tripped. He tried to catch her, but she was off-balance from her narrow skirt. He moved, intending to brace her fall. His foot got caught in her long train and he went down, Leighton falling onto his chest. After the initial rough contact, air pushing out of both of their lungs, Axl was not disappointed in the position. Her chest was spilling out of the dress, giving him a hell of a view.

"Talk to me," he said. "What's going on?"

But Leighton shoved off of his chest, hauled herself to her feet and took off again. For a second he lay there wondering what the hell he was supposed to do now. Then he jumped up because damn it, she was going to talk to him. She was going to listen to him.

Because he was falling in love with Leighton and she had to hear it from him.

So he reached her for the second time. Only this time he didn't give her an opportunity to escape. He bent his knees, picked up Leighton with one arm under her ass, and threw her over his shoulder. She was shrieking and kicking. He ignored her and marched her down to the dock. He stepped onto Bill's boat, knowing the keys were always under the seat, and plunked her down on a cushion.

"What are you doing?" Leighton asked, looked indignant.

At least her panic seemed to have receded.

"I'm taking you out on the lake so that I can tell you how I feel without you running away." He fired up the motor and untied the boat. A minute later they were pulling away from shore.

Leighton threw her bouquet at him. "Let me off this boat!"

It was so unlike her he just stared at the flowers after they bounced off his chest and tumbled to the ground.

He hoped someday this would be a funny story about how he had kidnapped his bride.

Right now he had no clue how any of this was going to shake out.

"You look beautiful," he told her. "I like the dress." He reached out automatically and drew a finger across her shoulders. She let him, which made him smile. "And I like you."

.   .   .

LEIGHTON WANTED TO KICK AXL. He was smiling. Like this was all so damn funny. She was miserable, her heart breaking, and he was smiling. She sat on the bench and crossed her arms over her chest. Bill's lawn was crowded with wedding guests, all staring at their departure. Their voices, all in shocked tones, were creating a collective hum. She couldn't understand what anyone was saying but it was clear her dashing off had rocked the crowd.

She had flat-out panicked, then Axl hadn't given her the answer she wanted, and now she was both broken-hearted and humiliated and she wanted to kick him in the crotch for making her fall in love with him.

Glancing at the water, she briefly debated jumping overboard but with the wedding gown on, she'd sink like a tank. On the heels of that thought, she considered taking the gown off first but then she would arrive on shore dripping wet in slutty underwear with fifty people watching her. No thanks.

She was stuck.

Axl didn't go very far before he cut the engine. He turned to her. "Can you please tell me why you're running away?"

"I told you," she said, and her voice cracked. "I can't do this. It's not right. I don't give a shit about my job anymore if it means I have to stand there and say 'I do' to you when the truth is..." She took a deep breath and laid it all out there. She wanted Axl to know how she felt. "A part of me wishes we were really doing this. Getting married. Because I really, really care about you."

Axl came over to her and sat down on the bench next to her, the movement sending the boat rocking gently. "Leighton." He stared into her eyes, running his hand over her glossy beach waves.

She steeled herself to be let down easily. To be told that she was getting a participation ribbon, but no prize.

"If you had let me finish," he said, "I was going to tell you

that while today might not be real, it could be at some point."
He kissed her softly.

Leighton trembled at the touch. "What do you mean?" she murmured.

"I mean that maybe this could be us in two years or a year, or hell, nine months from now. Six months. Because this week I found something I didn't even know I was looking for—you."

Her heart swelled. "Really?"

He nodded. "Really. I am crazy about you. In fact, I think I might be falling in love with you. As insane as that sounds."

"It is insane. But I feel the same way." Tears blurred her vision of his handsome face.

"You do?" He gave an exhalation of air from his nostrils.

For the first time ever it occurred to her that Axl might have the same fears about putting his heart on the line as she had. It made her feel tender toward him and overwhelmed with love.

"I do," she told him, fully aware of the irony of those words. She leaned into him, gripping the front of his tuxedo shirt so she could give him a soft kiss. "I never thought, in a million years, that a guy like you, with a girl like me..."

He cupped her cheeks and he kissed her over and over. "Hey, California, haven't you noticed that we have very similar personalities? It could work, you know. You and me. I want it to work."

"Thank you for not wanting to change me," she said, and she meant that with everything inside her. "For thinking that I'm enough."

"You are more than enough. You're everything."

Her heart swelled to the point she thought it might explode.

"And hey, I want you to know I appreciate that you see in me stuff no one else does. That you think I'm, you know, normal."

She'd never seen him look vulnerable but he did now. The

marine turned cop had his own insecurities, she realized. She gave him a soft kiss. "Axl, there is nothing abnormal about you at all."

"What do we do now?" she asked, when he didn't seem inclined to do anything other than brush his lips over hers again.

"I say we cancel the wedding and figure out how we can date long distance and really get to know each other."

It sounded like a plan to her. "Do you think that will work?"

"It will if we want it to." He ran a finger over her bottom lip. "You look stunning, by the way. You blew me away. For a second, I couldn't breathe when I saw you."

She believed him, and it was the greatest, most amazing compliment. She felt her cheeks burn. From modesty, arousal. From love. "Thank you. You wear a tux well. You're the hottest groom I've ever seen." She meant that.

"I am so turned on right now by you, by knowing you care about me. Does that make me an asshole?"

She laughed. "No. I'm sitting here hoping we can still have a wedding night, even without the wedding."

His eyes darkened. "Hell yeah."

"I guess I'm going to get fired," she said, wrinkling her nose. "And I don't even care."

"Maybe not. This right here." He gestured to each of them, to the lake, and their guests. "This is TV gold. You can't even write this shit."

He probably had a point. "I guess we have to go back."

"I could start the engine up and we can just drive. Go to Canada and have a fake honeymoon in a cabin in the woods."

It was tempting. "As much as I'd love to, I think we might owe everyone some sort of explanation."

"You mean telling everyone go home doesn't cut it?" He gave her a grin.

"No." Leighton shook her head at him. "Now drive, Ice Man."

"Ten bucks says they start calling you Runaway Bride at work."

Leighton laughed, her heart full. She was so happy to be with Axl, she didn't even care. "They can bring it. I'm ready. I'm not going to keep my job anyway. I kind of think there might be other options I'd like to explore. Maybe a floral shop or a tea shop or a dress shop. In Minnesota. At some point."

The look he gave her set her inner thighs aflame.

"I'm ready too then," he said.

FOURTEEN

"I'M NOT GOING TO LIE," Jesse said, standing by the bar under the tent. "This is the best wedding I've ever been to."

Axl laughed. "Thanks, man." After apologizing to everyone there wouldn't be an actual wedding, they had made the decision to go ahead with the dinner and dancing. It was all paid for, no reason not to enjoy it. Especially since he and Leighton weren't ending a relationship. They were just getting started.

"Hey," Sullivan said, raising his hand to the bartender for another drink. "I had an awesome wedding."

"No offense, bro, but we were like twelve when you got married," Jesse said. "I got so shit-faced I don't even remember your reception. Restraint was not in my vocab in those days."

"Yeah, you were so restrained when you took Leighton's friend home last night," Brandon said, rolling his eyes.

"I remember it, at least. So I'm maturing."

"Why is Sloane crying?" Axl asked, sipping a beer. She and Rick were coming into the tent and Sloane wasn't just crying, she was sobbing.

Sullivan stood up straight. "What did that fucker do to my sister? I'll kick his ass."

But Sloane came running over to them and stuck her hand out. There was a ring on it. "Rick proposed to me!"

Rick was grinning ear-to-ear. "She said yes," he said, sounding proud and ecstatic.

Axl clapped him on the back. "That's awesome! I'm happy for you guys." He gave Sloane a hug. "Congrats, you crazy kids."

"I wasn't planning to propose tonight because I didn't want to ruin your wedding, Axl, but then you called it off and the setting is pretty damn romantic. I hope you don't mind."

"No, not at all. It is a great setting. How did you have the ring though?"

"I've been driving around with it in my glovebox trying to figure out the perfect way to ask Sloane." He shrugged.

"I don't know," Jesse said. "Sloane is crying. I think you fucked it up."

"Shut up," she said, hitting Jesse's arm. "You know these are happy tears." She turned to her brother. "Aren't you going to say anything, Sullivan?"

He gave her a one-armed hug. "Congratulations, Sloane. I'm really happy for you, seriously." Without a word to Rick he took his drink and walked off.

Sloane sighed.

"Baby, don't let it bother you," Rick told her.

"I know." She wiped her cheeks. "I'm going to find Lilly and show her my ring."

They kissed and then she walked away.

"Married. Damn," Brandon said. "I'm happy for you guys. Things are changing, aren't they?"

Axl saw Leighton laughing under the glow of chandeliers, dancing with his five-year-old nephew. His heart did a flip. "Yeah. Things are changing."

Setting his beer back down on the bar, he crossed the tent, making his way across the dance floor. As if she sensed his presence, Leighton turned when he was still ten feet away, and gave him a look so filled with love and lust that his nostrils flared. Damn. He was a lucky fucking man.

She didn't seem to mind eyes being on her now. She looked relaxed and happy, confidence in what they were doing. And herself. It made him even happier to see that. She raised her eyebrows as he approached.

"Beat it," he told his nephew Sam in teasing tones. "I'm cutting in."

"No!" Sam said, sticking his tongue out at him.

"Go have a piece of cake," he told him, amused by how disheveled Sam looked, his shirttail out and his hair sticking up in a persistent cowlick.

"Mom said I can't have another one."

"But this is my wedding and I said you can, so go for it, kid."

"Really?" Sam's eyes got huge.

"Really."

Sam ran away.

"Nice," Leighton said with a soft laugh. "Bribing children."

He shrugged. "It worked on me as a kid. Will you dance with me?"

"I would love to dance with you." She took his hand and moved in close against his body.

He would never get tired of the feel of her curves pressed against him. Swaying with her to the music, he leaned down and kissed her softly.

Then because it felt right, he stared into her eyes. The words came easily, without thought. "I love you."

Her eyes widened. "I love you too."

It was a pretty freaking awesome reality.

Thanks for reading STRIP SEARCH! I hope you enjoyed Axl and Leighton's story.

Want more of the sexy TAP THAT guys?

STRIP TEASE is out with Brandon!

A sexy CEO.
A single mom.
And a secret baby who is now eight years old...

A tipsy night in college resulted in Grace's greatest joy--her daughter.

But now she sees the guy who gave her a fake name and number that night is stripping for a charity event without a care in the world.

When the feisty brunette confronts Brandon, finding out he has a daughter rocks his playboy world.

Grace wants answers.
Brandon wants Grace.
And Fallon wants a dad.

Is the ultimate party guy ready to strip it all bare...including his heart?

ABOUT THE AUTHOR

USA Today and New York Times Bestselling author Erin McCarthy sold her first book in 2002 and has since written over seventy novels and novellas in romance and mysteries. Erin has a special weakness for tattoos, high-heeled boots, Frank Sinatra, and dive bars. She lives with her husband and their blended family of kids and rescue dogs.

Connect with Erin:
www.erinmccarthy.net

ALSO BY ERIN MCCARTHY

Tap That Series